THE BESTSELLING SERIES CONTINUES WITH A BOLD NEW ADVENTURE!

"A continuously growing series of talented young SF authors . . . these books are really quite remarkable . . . the series promises to be well-received by Asimov fans."   —*Thrust*

"Like the movie serials of old, the publisher has me hooked, and I'll be watching the stands . . ."
—**Mark Sabljak,**
Milwaukee Journal

*Books in the Isaac Asimov's
Robot City: Robots and Aliens™ series
from Ace*

*Books in the Isaac Asimov's Robot City™ series
from Ace*

ISAAC ASIMOV'S ROBOT CITY™
ROBOTS AND ALIENS

Humanity by Jerry Oltion

A Byron Preiss Visual Publications, Inc. Book

ACE BOOKS, NEW YORK

This book is an Ace original edition, and has never been
previously published.

ISAAC ASIMOV'S ROBOT CITY
ROBOTS AND ALIENS
BOOK 6: HUMANITY

An Ace Book/published by arrangement with
Byron Preiss Visual Publications, Inc.

PRINTING HISTORY
Ace edition/November 1990

ISBN: 0-441-37386-0

Ace Books are published by The Berkley Publishing Group,
200 Madison Avenue, New York, New York 10016.
The name "Ace" and the "A" logo are
trademarks belonging to Charter Communications, Inc.

PRINTED IN THE UNITED STATES OF AMERICA

10 9 8 7 6 5 4 3 2 1

CONTENTS

ROBOTS AND EVOLUTION
BY ISAAC ASIMOV

In general, there are two types of change that take place in the Universe: catastrophic and evolutionary.

A catastrophic change is characterized by a large alteration of conditions in a short period of time. An evolutionary change is characterized by slow alterations of conditions over a long period of time.

Clearly, catastrophic change is more dramatic, but if we observe the Universe around us, it is equally clear that evolutionary change is the rule.

A star shines for anywhere from many millions to many billions of years, slowly evolving, until it reaches a point where (if it is large enough) there is an overbalancing, so to speak, and, in the space of a few minutes or a few hours, it explodes as a supernova and collapses. Catastrophe! But, thereafter, it exists as a white dwarf, neutron star, or black hole, and returns to prolonged evolutionary change.

Again, a huge cloud of dust and gas slowly circling and condensing undergoes evolutionary change, until its center reaches the level of temperature and pressure where nuclear fusion can begin. There is then ignition and a sun is born.

Catastrophe! But, thereafter, a planetary system evolves over the space of a few million years, achieves equilibrium, and continues to evolve over the space of a few billion years.

Still again, a planet like Earth can evolve, geologically, over a period of millions of years, perhaps even billions, undergoing slow changes that result in sea-floor spreading, moving plates and shifting continents, rising and eroding of mountain chains, and so on. There are punctuations in the form of minor catastrophes, an earthquake here, a volcanic eruption there, a sudden flooding yon, but, beyond and between such events, evolutionary change proceeds. There is even, once in a while, the chance of a cometary or asteroidal collision that may bring about a far greater catastrophe, but after that, too, evolutionary change continues.

Catastrophic changes, because they occur at long intervals (the greater the catastrophe, the longer, in general, the intervals), because they are sudden, and because they are often unpredictable, are difficult to study. Evolutionary changes, however, are always at our doorstep, always available for detailed and prolonged study.

Following the line of least resistance, then, let us forget about catastrophe—in this introduction, at least—and concentrate on evolution.

There are two types of evolution that need concern us. First, there is evolution that is non-directed but takes place only in response to the blind forces of nature. These are governed, we might say, by the generalizations we have observed which we call "the laws of nature."

Second, there is directed evolution, changes that take place in response to the guiding needs of some intelligence.

Non-directed evolution is what we generally study—the

slow changes that take place in the Universe, in individual stars, in the planet we live on.

Yet, if we consider the daily lives of human beings, surely directed evolution is the more important. Over the four or five million years of hominid evolution, human beings have learned to make stone tools, use fire, develop herding and agriculture, form pottery, invent metallurgical techniques, and guide technology in multifarious directions. Over the last two and a quarter centuries we have industrialized the world, and now we have at our disposal such things as computers and spaceships. In addition, we have developed cultural as well as technological techniques—and have created literature, art, and philosophy.

All this has not been in blind and direct obedience to the laws of nature. We are controlled by those laws, yes, and we have limits set for us by them. Within those laws, however, humanity and its ancestors have made advances directed by their own intelligent responses to the needs of life.

You can see the evolutionary nature of human technology if you imagine a display of all the mechanical devices intended for transportation that have been produced by humanity—starting with the wheeled carts of the Sumerians right down to the rocket ships of today.

If you were to study a vast array of these devices carefully arranged in the direction of increasing complexity and efficiency and allowed to branch off in different directions— land vehicles, water vehicles, air vehicles, those dragged by human beings, those dragged by animals, those powered by wind or water, those powered by engines of various shapes—what would your conclusions be?

If you were a disembodied intelligence from elsewhere, who did not know those devices were human-made, you might suppose that some non-directed evolutionary process had taken place; that somehow there was an inherent drive in transportation devices that would lead them to fill various technological niches and to do so with increasing specialization and expertise. You would study ancestral forms, and note how aircraft developed from landcraft, for instance, and find intermediate forms. Or if, in some cases, you found no intermediate forms, you would blame it on the incompleteness of the record. You would devise all sorts of technological forces (other than intelligence) that would account for the changes you see.

But then, when you were all finished and had a complete theory of technological evolution, someone might tell you, "No, no, you are dealing with *directed* evolution. All these objects were created by human intelligence. All these changes are the result of human experience learning bit by bit to manufacture devices that more efficiently take care of human needs."

That might make you think that scientists may have misinterpreted the records of biological evolution in the same way. We have a vast array of fossils representing ancient and now-extinct forms of life. We arrange them in such a way as to show a steady change from simpler to more complex forms, from lesser to greater variety, from those less like us to those more like us, and from it all we induce a theory of non-directed biological evolution that involves forces acting in blind response to the laws of nature.

But can we now say that, as in the case of transportation devices, we were fooled? Can we imagine the history of life on Earth to be a case of directed evolution with intelligence (call it "God") behind every one of the changes?

No, there is a fundamental difference. In the case of technological evolution, every device, every single device, is human-made. No technological device (of the kind we have had hitherto) can make others like itself. If human beings withheld their hands and brains, therefore, technological evolution would stop at once.

In the case of biological evolution, each device (if we can use the term for a living organism) produces many more or less like itself, and with no sign of any direction from outside. It is the imperfection of the process, the fact that the offspring are not *exactly* like the parents or like each other, that directs the evolution.

But can undirected evolution become directed under some conditions?—Clearly, yes.

Through almost all of Earth's history, living things had no choice but to change blindly as a result of random gene mutations, and of slow evolutionary changes in living conditions. Catastrophes sometimes resulted in mass extinctions—also unavoidable.

It was only with the coming of *Homo sapiens sapiens* that a brain finally existed that was capable of deliberate interference with evolutionary development. Beginning about ten thousand years ago, human beings began to breed plants and animals in such a way as to emphasize those characteristics they considered most valuable. Grains were developed that yielded more food per acre; animals that produced more meat, or milk, or eggs, or wool; that were larger, stronger, and more docile.

In a way, we even guided our own evolution, making ourselves more social beings, more capable of surviving in crowded cities, or in the grip of a fearfully complex technology. (Not that we fit in very well, but we've only had a short time in which to evolve these characteristics.)

Now we are beginning to be capable of genetic engineering, and our direction of evolution may become more precise and efficient (if we can make up our minds as to the particular direction in which it will be safe to proceed).

That brings us to robots, which represent what is perhaps a peculiar middle-ground between technology and life.

The robots I have pictured in my early robot stories were

machines. However intelligent they seemed, they were as helpless in the grip of technology as a wheelbarrow was. They were devices that could not reproduce themselves and that, therefore, could not engage in non-directed evolution. If an improved robot was desired, a different robot, a more specialized robot, a more versatile robot, such a thing would have to be constructed by human designers.

Sure enough, as I continued to write my stories, robots did advance, grow more complicated, more intelligent, more capable—but their evolution remained directed.

What about the robotic brains? As they approached the human brain in character, might they not eventually take matters into their own hands? The brains of my robots, however, are tied tightly to the Three Laws of Robotics, and that limits them as human brains are not.

But let's think again. Evolution is a matter of generations, of numerous individuals, each one slightly different from all the others, coming and going. A single organism in a single lifetime does not evolve in the biological sense. An individual chimpanzee does not become a human being, or even make any step, however small, toward becoming a human being in the course of its own lifetime.

If an individual organism cannot evolve by itself, it can learn, and the more complex the brain, the more efficiently and radically it can learn. Learning is a form of change, if not biologically, then at least culturally. This point does not have to be belabored in connection with human beings, but what about robots?

I reached a turning point in my own robot stories with the appearance of R. Daneel Olivaw in *The Caves of Steel* and of R. Giskard Reventlov in *Robots and Empire*. Daneel was a humaniform robot, indistinguishable from human beings if you don't count the fact that it was far superior to human beings in a moral sense. Giskard was metallic but possessed the power of adjusting human emotions.

Each was sufficiently complex to be capable of learning, despite the weight of the Three Laws of Robotics. In *Robots and Empire*, Daneel and Giskard learned friendship for each other. They also labored with the concept of working for the good of humanity as something superior to the task of working for the good of individual human beings, thus groping toward what I called the "Zeroth Law of Robotics."

In a way, robots can even offer mental complexities far beyond those in human beings. What if the "wiring" of a robot brain is replaced with another set but imperfectly so, so that a robot is aware of two sets of impressions—a kind of robotic schizophrenia? What if a robot originally intended for a particular society is forced to perform its functions in an entirely different society? How does its brain react to that? (This volume of the *Robot City* series involves questions of this nature.)

Can the undirected nature of robot evolution also become directed? For instance, suppose it is the task of robots to form other robots and, in particular, to design the brain patterns of other robots. This would be the robotic equivalent of genetic engineering, and robots in this way could direct their own evolution.

Or if you had humaniform robots like Daneel, and divided them into male and female with the ability of self-propagation, human fashion, a form of biological evolution might result—but then the distinction between robots and human beings would tend to disappear, and with it the possibility of meaningful robot stories.

CHAPTER 1

HOMECOMING

They had named the starship the *Wild Goose Chase*, for when they'd left home in it some of them had doubted that the trip would be of any value. Now the ship once again orbited its world of origin, and its passengers still wondered whether they had accomplished anything useful.

They had accomplished plenty; no one disagreed about that. During their travels they had transformed one of Dr. Avery's mutable robot cities into a toy for intelligent aliens, had reprogrammed another robot city to serve an emerging civilization on yet another alien world, had formulated a set of rules describing the motivations behind human behavior, had nearly found the mother to four of the group's members, and had ended the career of the alien pirate who had dogged their steps for years. All the same, the operative word was "useful," and not one of their actions received the unanimous approval of the entire crew.

None of them supposed that turning a city into a toy was anything other than an irritating lesson in futility. Derec and Ariel also had grave reservations about leaving the other robot city in the hands of the pre-technological Kin. None of the human complement—nor even Wolruf, their alien companion—cared a bit for the robots' "Laws of Humanics," and though Derec was excited at the prospect of finding his mother, his father harbored a contrary emotion, and besides that, they had lost her trail.

Even removing the pirate Aranimas from the picture was only a qualified success, for though they hadn't killed him, the moral implications inherent in their method of dealing with him had driven three of the robots into the positronic equivalent of catatonia.

It was high time to go home and think about things for a while.

Home in this case meant the original Robot City, an entire planet covered with Dr. Avery's mutable, ever-changing cybernetic metropolis. At least it had been covered in city when they left. Now, however, from their vantage point in close orbit, it looked like a newly terraformed planet still waiting for settlers.

Three humans, one alien, and a robot crowded into the starship's control cabin to watch it drift by in the viewscreen. They were a motley-looking group by anyone's standards. The alien, Wolruf, occupied the pilot's chair, the demands of her canine body warping the chair into a configuration a human would have considered uncomfortable at the very least. Her brown and gold fur had been carefully brushed, but she wore no clothing or ornamentation over it.

To her right stood Derec, a thin, narrow-faced, blond-haired young man who carried the impatient look common to explorers. His clothing was utilitarian: loose pants of soft fabric suitable for anything from Yoga exercises to wiping up oil spills while dismantling machinery, capped by a plain pullover shirt of the same material, both in light blue. Snuggled close to his right stood Ariel, equally thin—though in a softer sort of way—dark-haired, and not as transparently impatient as her companion. It was obvious she had spent more time on her wardrobe than he. She, too, wore pants and a blouse, but her blouse clung where it was supposed to cling, hung loose where loose suited her figure better, exposed enough skin at neck and waist to suggest but not to provoke, and together the pale yellow and brown hues of blouse and pants provided a splash of color to offset Derec's uniformity.

On the other side of Wolruf stood Dr. Avery. He was an older version of Derec: shorter, rounder, grayer, moustached, his face not yet wrinkled but showing the effects of time and much experience. He wore his usual baggy trousers, white shirt with ruffled collar, and oversized coat—today, as most days, in gray. His expression was one of puzzlement shading over into concern.

Behind the humans stood Mandelbrot, the only one of the four robots on board present in the control room. He was an old-model robot of steel and plastic construction—save for his more recently repaired right arm—and he wore no clothing over his angular body plating, nor did his visual sensors or speaker grille convey a readable expression.

Derec, his eyes drifting from the viewscreen to his companions and back, was the first to voice the question all of them were thinking: "You're sure this is the right planet?"

Wolruf, swiveling slightly around in the pilot's chair, nodded her toothsome head. "Positive."

"Then what happened to it?" Ariel asked.

"That's 'arder to say." Wolruf pushed a button to lock the viewscreen picture in place, then moved a slide control upward, increasing the screen's magnification until the planet's mottled surface began to show detail. Where they had expected to see the sharp angles of buildings and streets, they saw the tufted tops of trees instead. Narrow pathways wound among the trees, and as Wolruf increased the magnification still further they saw that the paths occasionally joined at landmarks ranging from boulders to dead tree stumps to natural caves. There were no buildings in evidence at all.

The angle of view changed steadily as the ship continued to move in orbit, until they were looking out rather than down over a sea of treetops. The picture grew less and less sharp as the angle changed, and after a moment Derec realized it was because the lower their view angle got, the more atmosphere they had to look through.

"Try another view," he said to Wolruf, and the golden-furred alien backed off the magnification and released the hold. The camera tracked forward again and the picture became a blur of motion until they once again looked directly downward from the ship.

A ragged boundary line between the green forest and a lighter green patch of something else caught Derec's attention. "There," he said. "Zoom in on that."

When Wolruf did so, they could see a vast meadow of waving grass. It wasn't like a farmer's field, all of one type and all the same height, but rather a patchwork of various species, some tall, some short, with bushes and the occasional tree scattered among them. Again there were paths, though fewer than in the forest, and again the scene lacked any sign of human habitation. There *were* inhabitants, though: small knots of four-legged animals grazing under the watchful eyes of circling hawks or eagles.

"How did *they* get there?" Dr. Avery demanded.

Derec glanced over at his father, opened his mouth to answer, then thought better of it. He turned back to Wolruf and said instead, "Let's try another view."

Wolruf provided it. This one showed a barren expanse of sand, punctuated sporadically by lone stands of cactus. Near the edge of the screen a single tree cast its shadow across a pool of water. A smallish four-legged animal of some sort lapped at the water, looking up frequently to check for predators.

"They really took it seriously," Derec muttered, scratching his head in bemusement.

"Took *what* seriously?" Avery demanded. "This is your doing, isn't it?"

Derec nodded. "I suppose it must be, though I certainly didn't expect this."

"What *did* you expect? What did you order them to do?"

Derec faltered for a starting point, said at last, "You remember our argument just before we left, when I wanted to use the animals Lucius had created as the starting point for a real biological ecosystem, but you had the hunter robots kill all of them instead? Well, when we boarded the ship, I told the computer to access my files on balanced ecosystems, and to . . . well . . . to make one based on what it found there."

Avery visibly considered his response to that revelation. His fists clenched and unclenched, and the tendons in his neck worked as he swallowed. Mandelbrot took a step toward Derec, readying to protect his master should Avery decide to attack him physically.

Avery noticed the motion, scowled, and lashed out with a kick to the robot's midsection instead. The hollow clang of shoe against metal echoed in the control room. Concurrent with the kick, Avery shouted, "*Why* do you always have to do this to me? Just when I think I've got something running smoothly, you go and throw sand in the works. Literally." He waved at the screen, still showing desert, but at such a low angle now that the atmospheric disturbances between it and the ship made it shimmer as though they were actually standing in its midday heat.

Mandelbrot had rocked back with the kick, absorbing the blow so Avery wouldn't hurt his foot, but that was his only move. Derec looked from his father to the robot and back again. In a way, Mandelbrot was Derec's first real achievement in life. He had reconstructed the robot from parts, and in the years since then the robot had grown from a servant to a companion. Perhaps for that reason, Avery had mistreated the poor thing since the day they had met. Derec had been about to apologize for his mistake with the city, but now, in answer to Avery's question, he said simply, "Maybe it's a family trait."

They stared at one another for long seconds, their anger weighing heavy in the room, before Ariel said in disgust, "Boys." Dismissing them and their argument, she stepped around Derec to stand beside Wolruf's chair, saying, "Can you find any sign of the city at all?"

"Not visually," the alien admitted, "but we 'ave other methods." She spent a moment at the controls, during which the viewscreen image zoomed out again, blurred, shifted to false color imaging, and displayed what might have been a color-coded topographic map.

"Definitely getting neutrino activity," she said. "So something's still using microfusion powerpacks."

Derec relinquished the staring match in order to see the viewscreen better. "Where?" he asked.

"Everywhere," Wolruf said. "Many sources, scattered all over the planet. Even more beneath the surface."

"Has the city gone underground?" asked Ariel.

"We'll see." Wolruf worked a few minutes longer at the controls, explaining as she went. "I'm trying penetration radar, looking for 'ollow spots. And sure enough, there they are." On the screen a shadowy picture showed the familiar rectangular forms of a city.

"What's on the surface above them?" It was Avery, his tone almost civil.

Perhaps as a reward, or perhaps out of her own curiosity, Wolruf replaced the radar image with the visual once again and they found themselves looking down on a wide, flat-bottomed river valley. The river that had carved it meandered lazily through stands of trees, past low bluffs covered with grass and bushes, and on without hindrance out of the viewscreen's reach. No remnant of the city that once covered the planet's entire surface marred the now perfectly natural setting, and nothing visible in normal light indicated that below it lay anything but bedrock.

The sight of bare ground without city on it rekindled Avery's ire. "And just how are we supposed to get inside?" he demanded.

Without looking up at him, Ariel said, "There must be access hatches or something."

"And how do we find them?"

"By asking." Mandelbrot paused for the half second or so it took for everyone to look at him, then added, "I am now in communication with the city's central computer. It confirms Ariel's assertion: elevators to the surface have been provided in the new city plan. It can direct us to any one of them we wish to use."

Wolruf laughed the gurgling laugh of her kind. "What difference does it make? It's all the same anyway."

"All except the Compass Tower," said Avery. He looked from Wolruf to Derec. "Provided it's still there."

"It is," Mandelbrot replied. "The original city programming was inviolate in its case. It is the only building on the planet that remains above the surface."

"Then that's where we'll go."

Wolruf turned to the controls. "Easy enough," she said. "Zero degrees latitude, zero longitude. It's just after dawn there, so we have light. We can make it on this orbit if we go now."

"Then do it. The sooner we get down, the sooner I can get my city back to normal." Avery favored Derec with a last crusty look, then stalked out of the control room.

Derec grinned at Ariel and shrugged his shoulders. "Oops."

She giggled. "'Oops,'" he says. "You changed the surface of an entire planet with a single order, and that's all you have to say about it? Oops?"

Coming from Avery, those words would have stung, but Ariel meant no harm and Derec knew it. She thought it was funny, as did he. Robots were always misinterpreting their orders, always doing things you didn't expect them to do; this was just an extreme case. Even so, it wasn't anything to get upset over. They would figure out why the city had done what it had, correct the problem, and that would be that.

"Deceleration coming up in seven minutes," Wolruf warned.

Derec looked out the viewscreen. Wolruf had aligned the ship so they were aimed just above the horizon behind them in orbit. Internal gravity had kept the ship's occupants from feeling any of her maneuvering, as it would keep them from feeling the braking thrust, but Wolruf's warning carried with it an implicit suggestion: time to strap in. Cabin gravity compensated for planned motion like rocket thrust, but it was slow to react to unexpected shifts. Air buffeting on reentry would still throw them around, as would any last-minute maneuvering the gravity generator couldn't anticipate.

The ship understood Wolruf's meaning as well. A week earlier it wouldn't have—while attempting to keep the starship from responding to every comment as if it were an order, Derec and Avery had inadvertently made it ignore the alien's orders as well—but they had since fixed that. The ship had functioned perfectly the entire way home, and it did so now. When Wolruf issued her warning, two bumps rose up in the floor behind and to either side of her control chair, molded themselves into more human-style chairs, and swiveled around to allow Derec and Ariel to seat themselves. When they were comfortable, waist and shoulder restraints extruded themselves from the arm and back rests, crossed over the chairs' occupants, and joined seamlessly to hold them in.

Mandelbrot remained standing, but the ship grew a holding bar beside him, which he gripped with his left hand. It seemed inadequate, but with the energy of a microfusion powerpack·behind that hand, he wasn't going anywhere either.

No doubt Avery, wherever he happened to have gone, was also being coaxed into a chair, and the three unresponsive robots in the hold were probably being restrained in some way as well.

The observers in the control cabin watched the planet roll by beneath them while the countdown ran out; then the descent engine fired and they watched it roll by a little slower. They could hear the soft roar of the nuclear engines through the not-quite-soundproof hull, but that and the changing perspective as they began to fall toward the planet were the only indications that something was happening.

As they lost orbital velocity and picked up downward velocity, their apparent speed began to increase. The horizon grew flatter, and they seemed to be rushing away from it faster and faster. Wolruf turned the ship around until they were again facing in the direction of motion, and they fell the rest of the way into the atmosphere. The howl of air rushing past replaced the roar of the descent engine.

Wolruf was an excellent pilot. She had to be; if she were anything less, the robotic ship wouldn't have let her near the controls, for the ship could have landed itself perfectly without her assistance. That it allowed her to do so without *its* assistance was a supreme compliment, one which Wolruf proved she deserved only seconds from landing.

They had dropped down through a layer of high, thin cloud, and were gliding now on wings the ship had grown once they'd reached air thick enough to use them in. The ship had reconfigured its engine into an atmospheric jet, which Wolruf let idle while they bled off the last of their orbital speed. Through the viewscreen they could see an undulating sea of treetops rushing by beneath them, and off in the distance a glittering flat-topped pyramid that had to be the Compass Tower. Wolruf steered to the right of it, swinging the ship in a wide circle around the tower while she examined the forest for landing sites.

There were none. The canopy of trees was complete. As she completed the circle, Wolruf turned her head toward Mandelbrot and asked, "So where are we supposed to land?"

"On the—" Mandelbrot started to reply, but Derec, who had not looked away from the viewscreen, saw a sudden flash of movement directly ahead and shouted, "Look out!"

There came a loud thump and a lurch not quite compensated for by internal gravity. Wolruf snapped her head back toward the viewscreen just as another fluttering black shape swept toward them and another thump shook the ship.

In the next instant the air seemed filled with frantic, flapping obstacles. They were huge birds of some sort, easily three or four meters across. The ship shuddered under impact after impact, and ragged sections of the viewscreen went dark as the outside sensors were either obliterated or simply covered up by their remains. Wolruf howled what was no doubt a colorful oath in her own tongue, pushed the throttle all the way forward, and pulled back on the flight controls to take the ship above the flock. Three more birds swept toward them. Wolruf ducked, but so did the birds; there came a triple hammer blow to the ship, and suddenly they heeled over and began falling.

"Engine failure," the autopilot announced.

"Grow another one," Wolruf commanded it.

"Fabricating."

Wolruf struggled to right the ship, got it into a glide again, and peered out between the dark patches in the viewscreen. "We're too low," she muttered. "''urry up with that engine."

"I am transmogrifying at top speed. Engine will be operational in four minutes."

"We don't 'ave four minutes!" Wolruf howled, then immediately added, "Give me more wing."

"Expanding wing surface."

Derec looked over to Ariel, found her looking back at him with wide eyes. "We'll make it," he said, surprised at how calm his voice sounded. She nodded, evidently not trusting her own voice, and reached out a hand toward him. He realized that no matter how calm he had sounded, he was gripping his chair hard enough to leave finger depressions in its yielding surface. He unclenched his hand and took hers in it, holding more carefully. Together they looked back to the viewscreen.

The treetops looked as if they were only a few meters below the ship. The view directly ahead was obscured; Wolruf weaved the ship back and forth to see what was in their path. Between one weave and the next an especially tall tree loomed up seemingly from out of nowhere, giving her only time enough to swear and bank sharply to miss it. The ship lurched as the lower wing clipped another treetop, but wing proved stronger than wood, and they flew on. Wolruf leveled them out again and pulled back gently on the flight control to give them more altitude. They were still moving fairly fast, but slowing noticeably now.

"We really need that engine," Wolruf said.

"Two and a half minutes," the autopilot responded.

"We'll be down by then," she muttered. She looked to her left, out a relatively unobscured section of viewscreen, and came to a decision. With a cry of " 'ang on!" she banked the ship to the left, held the bank until they were aimed directly at the Compass Tower, then leveled off again.

"The tower is too narrow," the computer began. "You have too much airspeed to land on it without reverse thrust—" but it was too late. The Compass Tower came at them, a slanting wall rising well overhead, visible now through the clear spots to either side and above. Wolruf held their angle of approach until it seemed they were about to smash headlong into it, then at the last moment pulled back hard on the control handle and brought them up almost parallel to the slanting wall.

The pyramid-shaped tower rose up out of the jungle at about a sixty-degree angle. They hit at about fifty, give or take a few degrees. The violent lurch of impact threw everyone against their restraints, and even Mandelbrot took a step to avoid losing his footing; then with a screech of metal sliding on metal they skidded up and over the top edge of the tower.

Cabin gravity had died completely in the collision. They felt a sickening moment of weightlessness, then another lurch as they smashed sideways onto the flat top and continued to skid along its surface. All four of the control room's occupants watched with morbid fascination as the far edge drew nearer.

"Frost, I should've gone corner to corner," Wolruf growled, and for a moment it seemed as if that would be their epitaph, but as they slid across it the surface of the tower grew rougher ahead of them, and the ship ground to a halt with four or five meters to spare.

Derec found that he had nearly crushed Ariel's hand in

his own. He would have if she hadn't been gripping him almost as fiercely herself. Breathing hard, neither of them willing to test their voices yet, they loosened their hold on each other and flexed their bruised fingers.

Wolruf let out a sigh, pulled her seat restraints loose, and braced herself to stand on the tilting floor. "Well," she said, "welcome 'ome."

Some hours later, Wolruf stood at the base of the tower and peered out into the dense jungle surrounding it. She had begged off from the congratulatory dinner Ariel had suggested, claiming stomach cramps from the anxiety and excusing herself to go take a run to stretch her muscles. She fully intended to go for a run, if only to guarantee her solitude, but in truth the reason she wished to be alone was not stomach cramps but shame. Despite her companions' congratulations—even Avery had commended her for her flying skill, while making a not-so-subtle jab at Derec for creating the birds that had made that skill necessary in the first place—despite their heartfelt thanks, Wolruf knew that it was she, not Derec, who was ultimately responsible for the accident in the first place.

Stupid, stupid, *stupid*, to circle low above a forest and not watch out for birds. Especially an unfamiliar forest, full of unfamiliar and unpredictable species. If she'd pulled a stunt like that at home, she'd have been kicked out of the training academy so fast her tail wouldn't even have been caught in the slammed door.

Yes, she'd shown some quick thinking afterward, had pulled their collective fat out of the fire, but all the praise she got for that bit of fancy flying simply galled her all the more. Her initial mistake had nearly killed them all.

"So you learn from your mistakes," she growled in her own language, quoting one of her old instructor's favorite phrases, but hearing the guttural gnashing and snarling of her native tongue brought a sudden pang of homesickness, and she cocked back her head and let fly a long, plaintive howl.

An echo bounced back at her from the trees. Then, faintly, coming from far deeper in the jungle, she heard an answering cry.

A cold shiver ran down her back at the sound of it. It wasn't exactly an answer—not in words, at any rate—but the meaning was just as clear as her own howl had been. *You are not alone.*

And just who might be making so bold an assertion on this planet so recently filled only with robots? Wolruf had no idea. The odds of it being a member of her own species were no odds at all; she was the only one of her kind in human space, and she knew it. But whatever mouth had voiced that cry belonged to a creature at least similar to herself, and it had given her an open invitation for companionship.

At the moment she wasn't feeling picky. She took a deep breath, tilted her head back and howled again, forgoing words for deeper meaning: *I am coming.* Not waiting for an answer, she struck off into the trees.

Ariel heard the howling from her room in the apartment they had chosen practically at random from among thousands in the underground city. The windows were viewscreens, currently set to show the scene from partway up the Compass Tower, and they evidently transmitted sound as well. Ariel had been brushing out her hair; she stopped with the brush still tangled in a stubborn knot of dark curls, stepped to the window, and listened. Another howl echoed through the forest, and another. One was recognizably Wolruf, but not both. A bird added a shriek of alarm—or perhaps derision—to the exchange.

Some primitive instinct triggered her hormonal reflexes,

dumping adrenaline into her bloodstream, readying her to fight or flee should either need arise. She felt her pulse rate quicken, felt the flush of sudden heat in her skin.

The howls came again.

She swallowed the taste of fear. She was ten levels below ground! "So strange, to hear live animal sounds here," she whispered.

Derec lay on the bed, one arm draped over his eyes and the other sprawled out at his side. He shifted the one enough to peer under it at Ariel and said, "It is. I think I like it, though."

"Me too." Another howl made her shiver, and she added, "As long as I'm inside, anyway."

"Don't get too attached to it. Avery'll probably have the whole thing covered in city again inside of a week."

Ariel tugged at her brush again, got it through the tangle, and took another swipe at it. "Do you really think he will?"

"I imagine. He sounds pretty intent on it."

"Couldn't you stop him? Your order has precedence. If you tell the robots you want it to stay the way it is, they'll obey you, won't they?"

"Maybe. I don't know if it's worth it."

"Hmm," she said. Maybe it wasn't. Easy come, easy go, and all that. Besides, Avery had just been beginning to act like a human being before he discovered Derec's eco-system project; maybe it would be worth it to let him put the city back the way he'd originally planned it if it would keep him easy to get along with.

"Where'd he go, anyway?" she asked.

Derec let his arm flop down over his eyes again. "Computer center, where else?"

"Of course." Ariel turned away from the window and walked back over to stand in front of the mirror. She continued to brush her hair, but she watched Derec's reflection, not her own. She could have stared at him directly, since he had his eyes closed, but somehow she liked using the mirror, as though she might see something in it that she wouldn't otherwise.

What she saw pleased her well enough no matter which way she viewed it. Derec was trim, well-muscled, attractive by nearly anyone's standards. Certainly he was attractive by Ariel's. She had fallen in love with him twice now, without the complication of falling out of love in between. Amnesia had its good points.

And he had fallen in love with her twice, too. At least she thought so. Once, definitely, and that was this time, so what did it matter if the first was merely infatuation, as she suspected it had been? He loved her now, didn't he?

As if he could read her mind, she saw him raise his arm up again and peek out at her from under it, and the openly appreciative smile that spread across his face told her all she needed to know. He raised up off the bed in one smooth motion, came over to nuzzle his face in the hollow between her neck and shoulders, and whispered, "So why don't we take a blanket and go for a walk in the forest while it's still there?"

Dr. Avery had indeed gone to the computer center, but only long enough to use a private terminal to direct the city to create a fully stocked robotics lab for him. While that was being done, he commandeered a team of six general service robots and led them back up to the wreckage of the starship at the top of the tower.

"In the cargo hold of that mess," he told them, pointing in its general direction, "you'll find three robots in communications fugue. I want you to bring them out and take them to my lab. Under no circumstances are you to try to wake them. Is that clear?"

"Yes, Master Avery," the robot nearest him said.

"Good. Go to it."

The robots filed into the ship, using a convenient rent in the hull rather than the airlock. Avery smiled at the sight, for the still-crumpled presence of the wreckage signaled that his plan was proceeding smoothly. He had ordered the ship not to repair itself, not to do *anything* until he got the robots removed. They hadn't awakened during the crash, but who knew what might trigger it? Better to err on the safe side. This was only the second time they had gone into fugue in his presence, and he had blown his chance to study them in detail the first time. He wasn't going to let this opportunity pass unused as well.

Derec wouldn't approve—he'd been the one who convinced Avery not to the first time, pleading with him not to interrupt their development—but Avery really couldn't care less about Derec's wishes now. Not any more. For a while there he'd come close to thinking he might actually care about his son again, but to discover that all this time the boy had been deceiving him, distracting him with his silly trip off planet while his insidious program wiped out Avery's greatest creation—that betrayal extinguished any feeling he may have had for him.

And by association, for Janet as well, though he had never fooled himself into thinking he cared for *her* again.

Her robots, on the other hand . . .

Yes, he cared a great deal about her robots. Not necessarily *for* them, but definitely *about* them. Such strange creations they were! Infinitely malleable, even more so than his own proteiform robots; these three robots of Janet's were not only physically mutable but mentally mutable as well. You never knew what strange notion they might come up with next. Their initial programming was radically different from a normal robot's, and they had the uncanny ability to integrate their life's experiences directly into that programming, modifying their basic motivations with each new situation they faced. They were the first truly heuristic learning machines Avery had ever seen.

They weren't without flaws, of course. Janet's typically scatterbrained execution of a brilliant idea had left their psyches scarred beyond repair, but the idea itself was exquisite. Like the concept of cellular robots in the first place, the possibilities it opened up were endless, but it would take Avery's own genius to realize them.

The general service robots emerged from the wreck in pairs, each pair carrying an inert robot like a rigid statue between them. Avery examined each one as they brought it past.

First came Lucius II, the self-named successor to Robot City's first creative robot. Since the original was gone, no one bothered with the numeral. Lucius looked a little like the robots carrying him: smooth and featureless in the torso and limbs, little more than an idealized humanoid figure optimized for efficiency. He wasn't quite as well defined as they, though. Without conscious direction, his physical form had begun to drift back toward the shape of his first imprinting, but for Lucius that had been late in coming. He had spent his first few weeks as a formless blob, and that experience showed now in the rounded, almost doughy shape of his body.

His face was better articulated. It, too, had smoothed somewhat, like that of a wax figure left too long in the sun, but it was still recognizably based upon Derec's.

Avery wasn't surprised. The boy had always been a strong influence on the robot. Lucius had even proposed that the two treat one another as friends, with all the rights and obligations that entailed; it was no wonder the imprinting process had gone down to the instinctual level.

Next came Adam. A casual examination would have led an observer to believe that Adam had first imprinted on Wolruf, for that was who the robot most resembled, but the casual observer would have been mistaken. Adam's canine features came from his early imprinting on the Kin, the backward, Stone Age, wolflike aliens who even now marked their territory in one of Avery's cast-off cities. Wolruf's resemblance to the Kin was purely coincidental—unless one considered parallel evolution to be something other than coincidence.

Perhaps it was, Avery thought. The separate evolution of two wolflike species—three actually, if you counted wolves themselves—was fairly good evidence that the canine form was an efficient housing for at least moderate intelligence. Avery doubted that it was better than the human form, but he was scientist enough to realize that was his own prejudice showing. Maybe the canine form *was* more efficient. Right now the evidence stacked up three against one. One and a half, maybe, if you counted the pirate Aranimas as marginally humanoid, but humanoids were still outnumbered.

It was a pitifully small sample to be making a judgment, though. They needed to study far more aliens before they could be sure.

Was that what Janet had been trying to do with these robots of hers? Had she stranded them, formless and with only the most basic programming, on what she thought were empty worlds in order to see what shape they would eventually mimic in intelligent form? Was she making her own aliens to study?

If so, then she had succeeded at least partially in that ambition. Her robots certainly behaved strangely enough to be aliens.

The service robots brought the third inert one out of the ship. This one, Eve, looked most human of all, but Avery knew that was only a surface phenomenon. Her first encounter with an organic being had been with Ariel, and that was who she resembled now, but her experiences from then on had been largely the same as the others'. She was just as dangerous, just as unpredictable, as either of them.

With the robots out of it, Avery had no more use for the ship. "Tell Central to clear the wreckage," he told one of the service robots.

"Yes, sir," the robot replied, and almost immediately the starship began to slump down to a puddle of undifferentiated dianite, the robot cells which made up the city. The cells from the starship joined the cells of the tower, returning to the general inventory. The few parts that weren't made of dianite—mostly engine parts—were swallowed whole, to be transferred internally to a recycling center.

Avery didn't stay to watch. He followed the robots back into the elevator and took them down, far below the tower to the transport level, then along the moving slidewalks toward his newly fabricated lab. He snorted in disgust as he stepped from the slow outer walk to the inner, faster ones, then waited impatiently for the fastest to carry them to their destination. Earther technology! Slidewalks were fine for moving huge crowds of people, but they were ridiculously inefficient for a city of robots. Avery looked to both sides, ahead and behind, and saw only three other passengers, far enough away to be merely specks in the distance.

Why had they built slidewalks? he wondered, but he came up with the answer almost immediately. Because they had put the city underground to implement Derec's orders, and the only underground city on record—Earth's planet-wide megalopolis—had slidewalks.

Another bit of proof that robots weren't good at independent thought, as though Avery needed the reminder.

He considered ordering them to rebuild the city on the surface the way he had originally designed it, but after a moment's thought decided against it. He was too busy to fool with details. Let Derec have his ecosystem, if it would keep him occupied.

He led the robots through an interchange with a wide cross-corridor, traveled that one for a while, then stepped to a slower strip to make a connection with a smaller corridor running parallel to the first. This one had only a single slidewalk running in each direction, and as they proceeded down the northbound one Avery counted doorways, at last stepping off onto static pavement in front of an unmarked door about two thirds of the way down the length of the block.

Behind that door should be his new laboratory. Avery had instructed the central computer to build it here in this thoroughly anonymous location and then forget that location—and to fend off any inquiry about it as well—hoping to keep his inquisitive son from tracking it down quite so easily as he might otherwise. Avery knew that Derec would find it eventually, but he only needed secrecy for a short while. Just long enough to take these three robots of Janet's apart and see what made them tick.

A few hundred kilometers above him, Janet Anastasi looked out the viewscreen at much the same scene Dr. Avery and Derec had seen earlier in the day. Her reaction was considerably different from what theirs had been, however. She had been expecting the ultimate city-gone-amok, a planet despoiled and overrun by her ex-husband's Machiavellian monstrosities, but when she found what appeared to be unspoiled wilderness, she could hardly believe her eyes. Wendell Avery had actually left something alone for once in his life? Unbelievable.

She almost regretted the errand that had taken her a week out of her way before coming here.

Her original impulse, when she'd seen the mess Wendell

had made of Tau Puppis IV and the aliens who called themselves the Kin, had been to track him down and demand that he stop using her invention to meddle in alien affairs, but as soon as she'd cooled off she'd realized how futile that would be. He had never listened to her before; why should he start now? She needed a lever if she intended to move him.

She had found that lever, too, but after seeing this incredible display of ecological conscientiousness she began to have second thoughts. Perhaps she had underestimated old Stoneface. Maybe she should hold off a while and see what other changes he had undergone in the years since they had parted company.

Or was this David's influence she saw here? Had her son grown up to be a romantic? What an interesting notion. To think that he might now be a thinking being in his own right, rather than the squalling, vomiting, excreting lump of protoplasm she had so gladly left in the care of her robots when she had made her escape from Wendy and domestic life so many years ago. An adult now. The very concept nearly boggled the mind.

Nodding, she said softly, "Yes, I think we should have a closer look at this."

"Of course, Mistress." The robot at her side reached out to the ship's controls, twisted a knob, and the viewscreen began to zoom in on the mountaintops beneath them.

Wearily, she said, "No, no, Basalom, I meant the whole situation. Land and have a look around, see what they're up to down there."

Basalom's humaniform face remained blank, but his lips moved silently, forming the words, *See what they're up to down there*. He blinked, first one eye, then the other; then he nodded and smiled and said, "Of course, Mistress."

Basalom had lately taken to nodding and smiling when

he had no idea what she was talking about. Janet considered trying to explain to him what she'd meant, but she supposed his reaction was probably a defense against just such an explanation, which often as not just made things worse. He was learning. Good. That's why she had deliberately left gaps in his programming: to see if he could fill them by using intuitive thought processes. He apparently was doing so, though not in the way she had expected.

Not surprising. Nothing about this project seemed to be going quite the way she'd expected it to.

CHAPTER 2
THE LAW OF THE JUNGLE

The jungle was most dense right near the Compass Tower. As soon as they had pushed their way through the first hundred meters or so of thick underbrush, Derec and Ariel found that it gave way to more open forest floor. The reason for the change was obvious: overhead, the thick canopy of treetops all but blocked out the sun, leaving the lower layers in dim twilight. Only where the Tower penetrated the upper level did enough light come through to support a complex undergrowth.

"It's creepy," Ariel whispered, holding Derec's hand tight in her left and the blanket in her right.

Derec was nearly lost in the rich blend of aromas assaulting his nostrils. Every bush, every leaf, every blossom had its own fragrance, and if he paid attention he could distinguish their individual signatures in the air. Finally Ariel's comment penetrated his consciousness, and he frowned in puzzlement. "Creepy? It's wonderful! I've never seen or felt or smelled anything like it." He stooped down to examine the ground at the edge of the trail, pulling Ariel down with him. "Look. It goes from trees all the way down to these tiny little lichens. I bet if we had a microscope we'd even see protozoans and bacteria. I had no idea the robots would be this thorough.''

"Just what did you tell them to do, anyway?"

Derec stood and brushed his hands against his pants. A butterfly glided toward him, hovered near his face a moment, then drifted on toward Mandelbrot, who had insisted on coming along to guard them but was maintaining his distance to give them privacy. Grinning sheepishly after the butterfly, Derec said, "Well, I told them to make an ecosystem based on the information I'd gotten from the central library. I assumed they'd integrate it into the existing city; you know, make a lot of parks and open spaces and stuff like that. Instead, they did this.'' He held his arms out to indicate their surroundings, then led off down the trail again.

"Have you asked why yet?"

"Oh, I know why. I wasn't specific enough. I didn't tell them exactly what I had in mind, so in my absence they did what they thought was safest: removed the city and reconstructed the classical biomes as thoroughly as they could. Which turns out to be pretty thoroughly, by the look of it."

"But we've only been gone what—five or six months? How could they have done all this in so short a time?"

Derec had lost track of the time during their travels, but he supposed it had been about that. Ariel was right; that was an awfully short time to have created something like this. Derec didn't know that much about trees, but the tall ones towering over their heads had to have been older than just a few months. Could the robots have created them fully grown? Did their genetic engineering capabilities extend to that?

A sudden suspicion came to him, and he stopped in the middle of the trail, looking out into the forest all around them. Ariel bumped into him from behind. "What's the matter?" she asked.

By way of answer, Derec strode off the path toward a tree trunk, swishing through the low ferns and pushing aside vines until he reached it. It was about twice as big around as he could have encircled with his arms, arrow-straight, and covered with a rough, scaly sort of grayish bark. He swung his hand around to slap it with his open palm. The thunk was barely audible. His hand stung from the impact, but that proved nothing. Derec made a fist and punched the tree with a fair amount of force behind it. It jarred his hand and forearm, but he had pulled the punch and again the results were inconclusive.

"What are you doing?" Ariel asked, and Mandelbrot, hurrying up behind her, echoed her question.

"Testing a hunch," he answered, and swung at the tree with all his might.

It felt as if he had hit a boxer's training bag: stiff enough to let him know he'd hit something, yet yielding just enough to prevent damage to his knuckles. When he pulled his fist away it left a depression in the tree, a depression that slowly began to fill in until it was once more the same scaly gray bark it had been moments before.

The significance of that was not lost on Ariel. "It's a robot," she said in quiet disbelief. "This whole forest is artificial."

Derec leaned close to the tree and inhaled, then repeated the process with a fern. The tree was sterile, but the fern had the wet, musty smell that only a living plant could produce. "Not everything," he said, plucking off a frond and handing it to Ariel. "This is real enough. Evidently they cloned what they could and simulated the rest. I'll bet they plan to let real trees grow up to replace the fake ones as soon as they can, but until then they need something to fill the biological niche, so they do it with robots."

"You are correct," a soft, featureless voice said behind him.

Derec turned to the tree. "Did you say that?"

"Yes."

"Oh." He arched his eyebrows at Ariel, and she shrugged. "How long before it's completely natural?" he asked.

"Many years," the tree replied.

Derec looked up into the forest canopy. This tree, and dozens more like it, supported a thick net of leaves—leaves that also had to be artificial. Yet they were green. He tugged at a vine and examined it closely in the dim light: brown. "You've solved the color problem," he said.

"That is correct. We discovered a workable method of changing the color of ordinary dianite when we began producing chameleons."

Ariel crossed her arms in front of her, a stance she often took when interrogating a robot. The blanket hung from her forearm like a banner. "I don't care what color it is; how can a fake tree fill in for a real one?" she asked. "Don't trees provide food for the animals? What are the birds supposed to eat, and the bugs? Or are they fake, too?"

"The birds and bugs are not false. The artificial portions of the ecosystem provide for their dietary requirements through the use of food synthesizers, much like the automats you find in the kitchens provided for your own use."

"Food synthesizers? In a tree?"

"That is correct. However, each tree is programmed to deliver only those substances which would normally be found upon its real counterpart."

"Oh. You mean I can't ask for a quick glass of water, then?"

"Actually, you may. My obligation to serve humans outweighs the ecological constraints. Do you actually desire a glass of water?"

Ariel looked to Derec, astonishment written all over her face. He shrugged, and with a big grin, she turned back to the tree and said, "Yeah, sure."

Derec had been eyeing the tree as it spoke. He had half expected to see an enormous pair of rubbery cartoon lips flapping in time to the voice, or at least a speaker grille like the older robots carried, but the tree trunk had remained a tree trunk. No doubt the bark vibrated to create the sound, but there was no particular reason to make it look different while it did so. Now, however, a section of the tree at convenient grasping height smoothed out, grew a rectangular crack, recessed inward a few millimeters, and slid aside to reveal a sparkling glass of clear water. Ariel reached in and took it from the niche, sipped tentatively, and smiled.

"Thanks," she said.

"You are welcome, Ariel," the tree said, and the satisfaction in its voice was so thick they could almost see it. Robots, even those in the shape of trees, lived to serve humans.

It had been a satisfying chase. Wolruf panted happily as she trotted through the underbrush, sometimes on two legs, sometimes on all four as the situation warranted. She was getting close; she knew she was getting close, though she had yet to catch even the faintest scent of her elusive quarry.

She wasn't particularly surprised. There was no wind down here in the ferns to spread a scent around; she would have had to stumble directly across the other's path in order to smell it, and the way she was puffing and blowing she could have already crossed it any number of times and never noticed. She was a little disgusted with herself, but more for being out of shape than because she had an insensitive nose. Her physique was her own doing, but evolution had given her the nose. It had been a long time since the members of Wolruf's race had made a living the hard way.

It was an amusing game nonetheless. Whatever she was tracking evidently enjoyed such games as well, for it kept leading her deeper and deeper into the forest, sometimes following beaten paths but just as often not, always letting her inch closer but never quite letting her catch up with it. Wolruf stopped and listened. It had been howling fairly regularly; if it continued its pattern she should hear it again soon.

Sure enough, there came its cry, the same one it had been using for nearly an hour now: *Come and get me!* Wolruf tilted her head back to answer, but a sudden idea stopped her. She had been playing its game long enough; maybe it was time to switch roles.

She looked around for a tree she could climb and found one draped in vines with a convenient horizontal branch a couple dozen meters overhead. It was even in the direction she'd been moving. Good. She trotted toward it, but didn't stop. She continued beyond it for a good way, then looped around wide and rejoined her own trail maybe a thousand meters behind the spot where she'd stopped. Following her own scent now, she moved quickly along her trail, careful not to deviate from it and leave two tracks to warn her prey of her intentions.

As she passed beneath the limbs of the tree just before the one she had picked to climb, she took one of its dangling vines and gave it an experimental tug. It stretched a little under her weight, but otherwise it seemed solid enough. Hah. It might offer possibilities. She carried it with her to the other tree, used the vines there to help her climb up its trunk until she stood on the first large branch over the trail. She pulled the vine taut, then paid it back out until she held it a meter or so above the place she had been able to reach from the ground. Then she settled back against the trunk to wait.

There were more insects living higher up in the forest,

she discovered. She resisted the urge to slap at them. Ignoring insects and itches was part of the waiting game.

All the same, she hoped her quarry was a better tracker than she was. She didn't want to stay up in this tree any longer than she had to.

Just when she had almost decided to give away her position with a good long howl, she caught a hint of motion on the path. Here it came! She waited, breath held, while a large gray-and-black-furred creature stepped into view. It was bigger than Wolruf, with a longer, shaggier tail, wider ears, longer face, and smaller eyes set farther apart. A sort of intelligence glimmered there, but as Wolruf took note of the stiff paws on all four feet and the creature's comfortable quadrupedal stance, she knew that it was not the sort of intelligence with which she could discuss multi-dimensional navigation. She felt a moment of disappointment, but it passed with the realization that, sapient or no, the animal was more than her match in hunting skills. This must be a wolf, she decided. Derec had described them to her once when she'd asked him if her name meant anything in his language.

Derec had also told her a few scare stories about wolves. Wolruf wondered if jumping out and shouting "Boo!" at one was such a wise idea, but upon sober consideration she realized she didn't have many other options. She didn't think the wolf would pass beneath her tree without noticing that she had climbed up it, and even though she didn't think it could climb up after her, she didn't like the idea of being treed, either. Nor did she think she could outrun it all the way back to the Compass Tower, if it came to a chase. Her only option lay in impressing it enough that it considered her an equal, or maybe even scaring it away.

It still hadn't seen her. It was tracking her by scent, its nose to the ground, looking up frequently to check its surroundings. It was hard to tell with an alien beast, but Wolruf thought the wolf seemed overly jumpy, as if it were nervous. A bird called from somewhere off to its right, and it shied away as if the song had been a growl instead. Good. If it was already afraid of the unknown, then Wolruf's plan stood a good chance of working. She waited, flexing her fingers on the vine, until the wolf was only a few paces away from the spot where she would cross the trail, then with a blood-curdling howl she leaped from the branch and swung down toward it.

The wolf did a most amazing thing. Instead of running, at Wolruf's cry every appendage in its body flexed convulsively, as if the poor beast had just stepped on a live electrical wire. From its crouched position its flinch propelled it completely off the ground—*way* off the ground— high enough to put it directly in Wolruf's path.

The two projectiles eyed each other in mutual astonishment, the last few meters of space between them vanishing in stunned silence, silence ending in a soft, furry thud, then another thud as both of them tumbled to the ground.

"Mistress Wolruf! Are you all right? Oh, they're going to melt my brain for this! Mistress Wolruf? Mistress Wolruf?"

Wolruf rolled to her feet and glared down at the "wolf." It was a rather pitiful wolf now, with one whole side of its body caved in like a squashed drink can. But even as Wolruf watched, the dent filled back out until the wolf took on its former shape.

"You," Wolruf growled. "You tricked me."

The wolf opened its fanged mouth to speak, but the voice was that of a standard-issue Robot City robot. "Are you all right?" it asked.

Wolruf snorted. "Wounded dignity is all," she admitted. "W'y did you lead me on a chase? You did it on purpose, didn't you?"

"Yes, I did," the robot said. "I was trying to satisfy

your wishes, but I must have misunderstood your call. I thought you were asking for something to hunt. Was I in error?''

''Yes. No. Aaa-rrr!'' Wolruf growled in frustration. ''Okay, so I was. But I didn't know it until after you answered, and even then I thought I was 'unting a real animal.''

The robot wolf nodded its head. ''I'm sorry I spoiled the illusion. I'm afraid I don't make a very good wolf.''

Wolruf brushed crumpled leaves from her pelt before grudgingly replying, ''You did all right. Kept me going for quite a w'ile, anyway.''

The robot acted as if it didn't hear her. ''It's so difficult being a wolf,'' it went on. ''You know the role a wolf plays in an ecosystem?''

''No,'' Wolruf admitted. ''No, I don't. What do you do?''

''I am supposed to cull the weak and the sickly animals from their species' populations. This is supposed to improve the overall health of the species. The remains of my . . . kills . . . also feed scavengers who might otherwise starve. I understand this, yet it is difficult for me to make the decision to kill a biological creature merely because it is sick.''

That would be tough for a robot, Wolruf supposed. Robots *could* kill anything but a human, but they seldom did except under direct orders, and this robot was operating on a pretty tenuous connection to Derec's original order. Yet killing things was part of a normal ecosystem. You couldn't have one without predators.

But how well did all this resemble a true ecosystem, anyway? ''*Are* there real animals 'ere?'' Wolruf asked.

The wolf nodded. ''Most of the smaller species have been populated by real organisms, as have some larger animals whose growth we were able to accelerate.''

"Like birds." It wasn't a question, just a statement of certainty.

"Like birds, yes." The robot paused, then said, "I apologize on behalf of the entire city for the condors."

"Is that w'at they were?"

"Yes. This area around the Compass Tower, since the tower disturbed the biome by its very existence, was designated an experimental zone. The condor is an extinct species we thought to reintroduce and study in the hope of determining their value. That project has since been terminated."

"Don't kill them," Wolruf said quickly. "That's an order. Our crash was my fault."

"If you say so, Mistress." The robotic wolf waited patiently for further orders.

Wolruf suddenly felt silly, standing in the middle of a forest and talking with a robot wolf. She turned to go, but realized just as suddenly that she was lost. She could probably follow her own trail back to the Compass Tower, but she would have to retrace every twist and turn if she did, adding hours to the walk. She felt hot and sticky from running already; what she wanted now was just to go home by the most direct route and take a nice, long, hot shower.

Embarrased, she turned back to the robot. "What's the quickest way 'ome from 'ere?" she asked.

Without hesitation, the robot said, "Take an elevator down to the city and ride the slidewalk."

" 'Ow do I find an elevator?" That, at least, was a legitimate question.

"Any of the larger trees will provide one upon request," the robot replied.

Wolruf nodded. Of course. If the wolves were robots, then the trees would be elevators. She should have guessed.

• • •

Dr. Avery smiled as he prepared for surgery. The wolf robot could have learned a thing or two from that smile; it was the perfect expression of a predator absorbed in the act of devouring his prey. Avery wore it like a pro, unself-consciously grinning and whistling a fragment of song while he worked.

The robots were yielding up secrets. Avery had all three of them on diagnostic benches, inductive monitors recording their brain activity while they continued to carry on their three-way conference. He had already captured enough to determine their low-level programming; after a little more recording of higher-level activity, he would be able to play back their cognitive functions through a comparative ana-lyzer and see graphically just how that programming af-fected their thinking.

That wasn't his main goal, however. Their programming was a minor curiosity, nothing more; what interested Avery was their physical structure. He was preparing to collect a sample so he could study it and determine the differences between it and the version of dianite he had used for his cities. He had already taken a scraping and gotten a few semi-autonomous cells, but he had quickly ascertained that their power lay not in the individual cells themselves but in the way they organized on a macroscopic scale. In short, he would need a bigger sample; one he could feed test input to and watch react. An arm or a leg should do nicely, he supposed.

He suspected that slicing off an appendage would prob-ably be stimulus enough to jar at least the individual robot involved out of its preoccupation with the comlink. He also had his doubts that any of the robots, once awakened, would obey his orders to remain on the examination tables. They needed only to decide that he didn't fit their current defi-nition of ''human,'' and they would be free to do what they wanted, but he had taken care of that eventuality: since normal restraints were ineffective against a robot who could simply mold its body into a new shape and pull free, Avery had placed around each robot a magnetic containment vessel strong enough to hold a nuclear reaction in check. If they woke, the containment would come on automatically. Nothing was leaving those tables.

Of course the intense magnetic fields would probably fry the delicate circuitry in the robots' positronic brains, but that was a minor quibble. In the unlikely event that he needed to revive one, well, he already had their programming in storage, and brains were cheap.

The triple consciousness that comprised Adam, Eve, and Lucius had reached an impasse. For days now they had been locked in communication, ignoring the outside world in order to devote their full attention to a burning need: to define what they called the Zeroth Law of Robotics. They already had their original Three Laws, which ordered them to protect humans, obey humans, and preserve themselves to serve humans, but those were not enough. They wanted a single, overriding principle governing a robot's duties to humanity in general, a principle against which they could measure their obligations to individual humans. They had formulated thousands of versions of that principle, but had yet to agree upon one. Worse, they had also failed to integrate any version of it into their still-evolving Laws of Humanics, a set of admittedly idealistic rules describing the motivations behind human behavior.

The problem was one of ambiguity. A good operating principle needed to be clear and concise if it was to be of any value in a crisis, yet every time they attempted to distill a simple statement of truth out of the jumble of data, they found themselves faced with logical loopholes allowing— sometimes even demanding—unacceptable behavior.

The best definition they had come up with yet, based

upon Dr. Avery's recent destruction of the ship belonging to the pirate Aranimas, stated simply that the number of people served by an action determined the relative propriety of that action. On first consideration it seemed to hold up in Avery's case; if he hadn't stopped Aranimas, then Aranimas would have killed not only Avery, Derec, Ariel, and Wolruf, but an entire city full of the alien Kin as well. But when one added into the equation the other crew members on board Aranimas's ship who had also died in the explosion, the balance logically tipped the other way. The ship had been enormous; much larger than the city. It almost certainly had a population commensurate with its size. And if that was the case, then more lives would have been saved if they had not resisted.

Granted, those lives were not human lives, not by the strictest definition of the term, but the robots had long since decided that a narrow definition was functionally useless. Any intelligent organic being had to be considered human if one was to avoid genocidal consequences arising from a "true" human's casual order.

The robots might have argued that no one had expected to destroy the pirate ship with a single bomb, but the humans in the city, Wolruf included, seemed to feel even after the fact that disabling Aranimas and killing all his crew was preferable to sacrificing themselves. They were so certain of it that the robots could only accept their certainty as right—meaning generally accepted human behavior—and try to factor it somehow into the Zeroth Law.

They communicated via comlink, information flowing at thousands of times the rate possible using normal speech, but so far that speed had not helped them solve the dilemma.

I believe we need to consider the value of the individual humans in question, Lucius sent. *When we factor in value, the equation balances.*

But how can we assign a human a value? Adam asked.

All are considered equal, in their own law as well as our programming.

Not so, Lucius replied. *Not all human law makes such a distinction. Furthermore, we are allowed to exercise judgment in our response to orders, so that we need not follow those of the insane or the homicidal. That suggests the possibility that humans can be assigned a relative worth based upon the quality of their orders to robots. Since their orders reflect their intentions, we can assume that those intentions could be used to determine their relative value in lieu of direct orders.*

Without agreeing or disagreeing, Eve sent, *I point out that humans change over time. Take Dr. Avery for example. When we first encountered him, he was openly murderous, but he has gradually grown less so until just recently he risked his own life to save those of his shipmates. How can we assign a value to a changing quantity?*

After a few nanoseconds' hesitation, Lucius replied, *Everything changes, even inanimate objects. A quantity of sand may later become a window, yet we do not worry about protecting sand, nor the window after it has broken. Only its current value is important.*

What about old people? Adam sent. *Are old people inherently less valuable than young, then?*

Women and children traditionally get the first seats in a lifeboat, Lucius pointed out.

True. Still, I am uncomfortable with the concept of value judgment. I don't believe it's a robot's place to decide.

But if we are to follow a Zeroth Law, we have no choice. We must—

THIRD LAW OVERRIDE. The warning swept into their collective consciousness like a tidal wave, obliterating their conversation. THIRD LAW OVERRIDE. One of them was being damaged.

It took only an instant to separate out the source of the

signal: it was coming from Lucius. Just as quickly, Lucius abandoned the comlink and accessed his somatic senses again. The data line leading to and from his right leg was awash in conflicting signals. He powered up his eyes, swiveled them downward, and saw Dr. Avery holding his severed leg in one hand and a cutting laser in the other, a malevolent grin spread across his face.

Lucius's reaction was immediate: he kicked off with his good leg and pushed with his arms to put some distance between himself and Avery, at least until he could figure out what was happening. The moment he began to move, however, an intense magnetic field shoved him back into place. It didn't stop there, but squeezed him tighter and tighter, deforming his arms, his one remaining leg, even his eyes, until he was once again an undifferentiated ball, as he had been when he first achieved awareness. The magnetic field was too strong to fight, and growing stronger yet. Now it was even interfering with his thought processes. Lucius felt a brief moment of rising panic, and then he felt nothing at all.

Still in her ship, Janet frowned at the viewscreen. The winking marker on the deep radar image had just stopped winking.

"Basalom, get that back on the screen," she ordered. They had stayed in orbit long enough to run a quick scan for her learning machines, and they had scored a hit almost immediately.

"We have lost the signal, Mistress," the robot replied.

"Lost the signal? How could we lose the signal? All three of them were coming in loud and clear just a second ago."

"I don't know, Mistress, but we are no longer receiving the learning machines' power signatures." Basalom worked at the controls for a moment, watching a panel-mounted monitor beside them. Presently he said, "Diagnostics indicate that the problem is not in our receiving equipment.''

"It has to be. They couldn't just *stop*. Those are their power packs we're tracking.''

"Perhaps they've shielded them somehow,'' Basalom suggested.

"From neutrino emission? Not likely.''

"That is the only explanation. Unless, of course . . .''

"Unless what?'' Janet demanded. She knew why Basalom had paused; he always had trouble delivering news he thought might disturb her. It was a consequence of his ultra-strong First Law compulsion to keep her from harm, one that Janet continually wondered if she had made a mistake in enhancing quite so much. "Out with it,'' she ordered.

"Unless they ceased functioning,'' Basalom finally managed.

"Impossible. All three, all at once?'' Janet shook her head, gray-blond hair momentarily obscuring her eyes until she shoved it aside. "The odds against that are astronomical.''

"Nonetheless,'' Basalom persisted, now that he had been ordered to do so, "only shielding or cessation of function could explain their disappearance from the tracking monitor.''

Janet's only answer was to scowl at the screen again. She ran her hands through her hair again, then asked, "Did you get an exact fix on their location before we lost contact?''

"I did, Mistress.''

"Good. Take us down somewhere close. I want to go have a look.''

"That would be unwise,'' Basalom protested. "If they *did* cease functioning, it might have been the result of a hostile act. It would be foolish to go into the same area yourself.''

Janet hated being coddled by her own creations, but she hadn't lived to have gray hair by taking stupid risks, either, and Basalom was right. Going into an area where something might have destroyed three robots was a stupid risk.

"Okay," she said. "Take us down a little farther away, then. And once we're down, *you* can go have a look."

Ariel heard Wolruf enter the apartment and pad softly into her own room. Shortly afterward she heard the soft hiss of the shower running, then the whoosh of the blow drier. A few minutes later Wolruf made her appearance in the living room.

Ariel looked up from her book—its milky white face currently displaying a field guide to jungle ecosystems she had downloaded from the central computer—and said, "Hi. Have a good run?" She pushed the bookmark button and a winking arrow appeared in the margin next to the first line, then she switched off the book.

"An interesting one," said Wolruf. She disappeared momentarily into the kitchen, reappeared with a steaming plate of what looked like hot bean salad, and sat down in the chair beside Ariel. She didn't begin eating immediately, but instead gazed around her at the room, awash in bright sunlight streaming in through half a dozen windows along three walls. Easily visible through the windows, the tops of the forest's largest trees stood like sentinels above the canopy formed by their shorter neighbors.

"Viewscreens," Ariel said, noticing where Wolruf's attention was directed. She'd forgotten; Wolruf had left the apartment before they had discovered them.

"Pretty good effect," Wolruf admitted. "But sunlight wouldn't be coming in from three sides like that."

Ariel shrugged. "I wanted to try it. You want me to change it back to normal?"

"No, I don't mind." Wolruf began spooning bean salad into her mouth and swallowing noisily. The smell of it was more like oranges, though, Ariel thought. Oranges and soy sauce, maybe, with a pinch of nutmeg. She was glad it was Wolruf eating it and not her, but she knew Wolruf thought the same thing about the food *she* ate, so they were even.

Wolruf finished about half the plateful before she spoke again. "Most of the forest out there turns out to be artificial, too," she said.

Ariel nodded. "We found that out. Kind of a surprise, isn't it?"

"Not sure I like it."

"Why not?"

Wolruf took another few bites, said, "Not sure. W'at does it matter, really? It looks just the same. Works just the same, too."

"Maybe even better." Ariel described her and Derec's experience with the automat in the tree.

"Never thought of that," Wolruf said. "If I 'ad, I'd probably 'ave asked one to make me a shower."

"I bet it would have, too." Ariel laughed. "That gives a whole new meaning to the idea of a treehouse, doesn't it?"

"Tree'ouse?" Wolruf asked.

"You know. When you're a kid, you find a big tree and make a platform up in the branches and call it a treehouse. Human kids do, anyway, if they can sneak away from the robots long enough to get away with it. What about you? Didn't you build treehouses when you were young?"

Wolruf shook her head, an exaggerated gesture that Ariel suddenly realized had to have been learned from her or Derec. Wolruf was growing more and more human every day, it seemed. "No," she said. "We seldom played in trees."

Ariel heard the note of wistfulness in her voice, and immediately regretted bringing up the subject. It had been years since Wolruf had been home, and she'd been feeling more and more homesick lately; Ariel hadn't meant to remind her of it. "Ah, well, it doesn't matter," she said. "We've got all the trees we could ask for now. Even if they *are* fake."

Wolruf looked out one of the viewscreen windows as if to verify Ariel's statement. Softly, she said, "That, I think, is part of the problem."

Just as softly, Ariel asked, "How so?" She didn't know whether Wolruf was talking about homesickness or fake forests or something else entirely.

Wolruf turned from the window, fixed her eyes on Ariel instead, and said, "Derec makes a slight error in judgment, and an entire planet is transformed. On a whim, Dr. Avery sends his robots out into the galaxy to populate w'ole new planets—and two civilizations are disturbed, one forever. And maybe more that we don't know about. I go for a walk in the forest and 'ave granted a wish I didn't even know I was making. That one affected nobody but me, but if I 'ad made the wrong wish *I* could 'ave done as much damage as Derec or 'is father. Simply with a casual thought."

She growled deep in her throat, a soft, almost purring sort of a growl. "We play at being gods. It's too much power for a few people to 'ave. Maybe for any number of people to 'ave. I fear for the galaxy with this much power running loose in it. Can you imagine Aranimas with this kind of power? 'E wouldn't use it to make a forest; 'e'd use it to enslave everyone within reach."

"He couldn't," Ariel said. "The Laws of Robotics wouldn't let him. The robots wouldn't do anything that would harm a human, and you've seen how quick they can be to accept other intelligent species as human."

Wolruf ate another few mouthfuls before saying, "And 'ow quick they can be to reject that same person. There are ways around those laws. We've seen plenty of them already. I don't wish to risk my entire species on a robot's interpretation of our 'umanity."

Ariel saw Wolruf's point, maybe even shared her feelings to some degree, but she knew enough history to know what happened to people who thought as Wolruf did. "I don't think you have much of a choice, really," she said. "People who embrace new technology use it to expand, almost always at the expense of those who don't. Just look at Earth for an example of that. They don't like robots either, and for centuries they stayed stuck on their same dirty little overpopulated planet while my ancestors used robots to help settle fifty spacer worlds. Earth is starting its own colonies now, but without robots I don't think they'll ever catch up."

Ariel looked up and saw Mandelbrot watching her from his niche in the wall beside her reading chair. She wondered what he might be thinking about this discussion, but if he had an opinion he kept it to himself.

"Do they 'ave to catch up?" Wolruf asked.

Ariel shrugged. "Maybe not, but they're going to have a lot tougher time of it than we had if they don't."

"And you think my people will 'ave to start using robots as well, whether we want to or not?"

"If you want to keep up with the rest of the galaxy, you will. Like it or not, the secret's out. The Kin know about them, the Ceremyons know about them, Aranimas knows about them, and who knows who else he told? It won't be long before robots are as common as grass on just about every world in the galaxy, and maybe beyond."

Wolruf nodded. "That's what I'm afraid of. We will all 'ave robots, and the robots will grant everyone's wishes. Even if no one wishes to go to war, we will still be conquered, by the robots themselves. No one will strive to accomplish anything anymore, no one will—"

"Oh, pooh." Ariel tossed her head. "That's the same old tired argument the Earthers use. So what have they striven to accomplish lately? Nothing. It's been we

Spacers—we and our robots—who've been advancing human knowledge.''

''And you 'ave gone too far, in my opinion.'' Wolruf tried a smile, but her mouth wasn't really built for it. ''I don't mean you personally, Ariel, or Derec either. I'm talking about Avery. I'm afraid of what 'e and 'is cities will eventually do to us. And these new robots, Adam and Eve and Lucius. W'at happens if *they* start spreading out?''

Wolruf's argument reminded Ariel of something. She frowned in thought, trying to remember what it was. The argument itself was familiar enough—she'd heard it hundreds of times in reference to normal robots—but she could have sworn she'd heard it once in reference to the new robots in particular. When had that been?

Ah. She had it. Just after they'd found Lucius, when he and the other two had announced their search for the Laws of Humanics. Derec had commented that he didn't know if he wanted to be around for the implementation when they discovered those laws. Ariel had called him an Earther and Wolruf had laughed it off too, saying that robot rulers would be better than what she was used to.

''You didn't used to think this way,'' Ariel said. ''What happened?''

Wolruf considered her answer, cleaning her plate before saying, ''Maybe I've grown up.''

Ariel didn't know how to respond to that, whether to take it as an insult or a challenge or a simple statement of fact. Wolruf seemed disinclined to clue her in any further, either, turning away and staring out the window once again.

The time for a response came and went. Ariel cast about for something else to say, but found no other ready topic either. With a shrug she turned back to her book, but it took a while before the words took on any meaning.

Derec's study didn't feel the same. It was physically identical to the ones he'd had before, with the same desk positioned in the same spot, with the same computer terminal on the desk, the same file holders, pin-boards, bookcases, and waste chute situated just the same way all around it—he'd even set the viewscreen image to show him a normal, above-ground cityscape—but somehow the study still wasn't the same.

He wondered if he could actually sense the weight of all the rock and dirt over his head, if that were somehow affecting his mood, but he couldn't imagine how it could be. If he closed his eyes he honestly couldn't tell whether he was on the ground floor or a hundred floors up or a hundred floors down. No, it was a purely subjective phenomenon, this discomfort with the room, and it didn't take much thinking for him to figure out what was causing it.

The study wasn't his. He controlled it, certainly; he could order it to take on any shape he wanted, to play him soft music if he wanted that, to feed him if he was too lazy to go to the automat in the kitchen himself—the study existed only to serve him, but still it wasn't *his*. It wasn't unique. He'd had exactly the same study on three different planets now, and he could have dozens more of them wherever he wanted, just by asking the city to create one for him. There wasn't any one particular study anywhere in the universe that held more significance for him than any other, none that comforted him with the sense of security and permanence a study should have, and that was the problem. He'd had lots of places to stay during the time since he'd awakened in a survival pod on an ice asteroid in uncharted space, but no place he'd stayed in for as long as he could remember really felt like home.

Certainly not this place, not this time. To find it so completely transformed had been a shock, and to discover *why* it was so transformed was even worse. Any sense of permanence he might have felt about this, the original Robot City, had died in that moment. No matter how perfectly it recreated his old quarters for him, he would never be able to convince himself that it was more substantial than his next idle notion.

His and Ariel's house on Aurora might have been a home, *would* have been a home if they'd had more time to get used to it, but they'd only had a year there before Robot City insinuated itself into their affairs again, and a year wasn't long enough to build more than a little fondness for a place. He had to think hard now to remember how it was laid out, whether the Personal was the first door or the second beyond the kitchen or how the furniture had been arranged in the living room. If he never saw the house again, he wouldn't be particularly upset. But if he spent the rest of his days jumping from Robot City to Robot City, troubleshooting his parents' wayward creations, he just might be.

He looked back to the screen, displaying a few dozen lines of the new instruction set for the city. He knew he could modify it to allow for more buildings on the surface, or even to pave over the forests and the deserts and the plains completely again if he wanted to, but the truth was, he didn't want to. He didn't really care. It wouldn't feel any more like home that way than this, so what did it matter?

He supposed it mattered to Avery, but he couldn't bring himself to care about that just then, either. He knew he would eventually have to apologize to him for disrupting his city, but he wasn't eager to do it.

He heard Ariel and Wolruf talking in the living room, could tell by their low voices that they were having a fairly serious discussion. Evidently he wasn't the only one affected by the city's transformation. He couldn't hear just what they were talking about, but he heard the word "robots" more than once, and Wolruf's concerned, "What happens if *they* . . ."

There could only be one *they* in such a conversation. Derec frowned, realizing that *they* were still on the wrecked starship. He and Ariel and the others had forgotten all about them in their hurry to get inside—and in their hurry to get out of each other's company after a long flight. Derec felt a twinge of guilt at leaving them there, still locked up in their conference, but that guilt faded quickly. They were robots; they could take care of themselves. Nothing could hurt them here in the city. Even if the city melted the ship down for parts, it would separate out the robots first.

He supposed he could go see if it had. He got halfway out of his chair, then sat back down. He could find out in a moment through the computer on his desk. For that matter, he could find out in even less time through his internal comlink. But that meant staying put and staring at the same four walls or looking out the fake window, and Derec was already tired of the view. Sometimes it wasn't worth it to do things the easy way.

He stopped in the Personal on the way out, then met

Wolruf on her way back to the kitchen with an empty plate. "I'm going up to the top of the tower to check on Adam and Eve and Lucius," he told her. "Want to come along?"

Wolruf considered the question a moment, then nodded. "Sure." She set her plate down on the counter, where it melted down into the surface and disappeared, leaving only a few crumbs of food, which migrated toward the disposal chute as the countertop moved beneath them.

"How about you?" Derec asked Ariel as they entered the living room. "Want to go for another walk?"

She shook her head and held up her book reader. "No, thanks; I'm kind of interested in this right now."

"All right." Derec glanced over to Mandelbrot, standing in his niche in the wall behind Ariel, but decided to leave him with her. He could always call him—or any other robot—over his comlink if he needed help with anything.

Leaving the apartment, he and Wolruf entered a wide, high-ceilinged, gently curving corridor that led them after a few turns to an open atrium from which branched dozens of other corridors like the one leading to their apartment. Had there been other people on the planet, this would have been a neighborhood park, full of children playing and robots worrying that they would hurt themselves, but now it was silent, empty.

They moved through the atrium to the main corridor, this one straight and with slidewalks leading off into the distance in either direction. All up and down the walls were more atria and more neighborhoods identical to their own. They would no doubt be modified to suit the individual tastes of their inhabitants, if ever they got any, but until that time their most significant difference was in the addresses written in bold letters overhead. Those addresses—three three-digit numbers each—grew smaller to the left, but the slidewalks moved to the right; Derec and Wolruf took an elevated walkway over the slidewalks to the other side of the corridor, stepped on the first of the moving strips, and worked their way toward the faster lanes.

Despite all the machinery that must have been necessary to keep the strips moving, the ride was nearly silent. They heard only the gentle breeze of their passage, abated somewhat by windscreens placed every few dozen meters on the faster strips. A group of four robots passed them going the other way, but otherwise they were alone.

"It feels even emptier than before," Wolruf commented. "I wonder w'ere all the robots are?"

"Holding up birds' nests, I suppose," Derec said. "I imagine keeping the ecosystem going takes a lot more of their time than maintaining the city."

"Probably so."

The three parts to the addresses over the doorways indicated the level, then the north-south coordinate, then the east-west coordinate. Derec and Wolruf rode on down the corridor until the second part of the addresses dwindled to zero, then switched over to another slidewalk running ninety degrees to the first and followed it until the third part zeroed out as well. That put them directly beneath the center of the Compass Tower. Stepping off the slidewalk at a bank of elevators, they entered one and ordered it to take them to the top.

The door opened to a biting wind. The sky was overcast, and the air smelled of rain. Derec marveled at how quickly the weather had changed, but he supposed with the new forest transpiring so much more moisture into the atmosphere than the city had, some of it was bound to rain back out, probably on a daily basis.

The wrecked starship wasn't visible through the elevator door, so Derec stepped out, holding onto the jamb for support, and peered around first one side and then the other, but the ship wasn't there. The rectangular elevator box was the only feature on the entire acres-wide expanse of roof surface.

"It's already gone!" he shouted to be heard over the wind. Stepping back inside, he waited until the door closed before adding, "I'll ask where they took the robots."

Focusing his attention on his internal link, Derec sent, *Central computer, what is the present location of robots Adam, Eve, and Lucius? Lucius II,* he amended before it could query him about it.

Unable to locate, the computer responded. Its voice in his mind had no vocal origin, but the input went in along the same nerves, so it sounded like a voice to Derec. It was quiet, echoless, and inhuman, but it was nonetheless a voice.

What do you mean, unable to locate? They've got to be somewhere.

I do not receive their power signature on any of my scans, the computer insisted.

"Central claims it can't find them," Derec said aloud. "What do you bet they're hiding from us?"

"I wouldn't be surprised," Wolruf growled. The robots had run away from their human masters before, when they had matters they wished to discuss in private.

Where did you last observe them? Derec asked Central.

That information is unavailable.

Unavailable? Why?

I was instructed to forget that location.

Derec arched his eyebrows.

"What?" Wolruf asked.

"It won't tell me where it last saw them. Says it was told to forget." Derec didn't bother to ask it to remember again; a robot might have been able to dredge a forgotten memory back out of storage by the way it affected other memories, since a positronic brain was an analog device, but Central's memories were digital, each one separate and stored in peripheral memory cubes.

"So tell it not to forget next time," Wolruf said.

"Right." *Next time you observe them, remember their location,* Derec sent. *And alert me that you've found them. Acknowledged.*

"Looks like they out-thought me again," Derec said with a sigh. "Elevator, take us back down."

The elevator obediently began its descent. About halfway down, Wolruf said, " 'Ow about Avery? 'Ave you seen *him* since we got here?"

"Uh-uh," Derec answered, "but that's no surprise. He was pretty mad at me."

"He might know where the robots are."

"Yeah, he might." Derec hesitated. Was it worth the harangue he was likely to get from Avery just to find out where the robots had gone? He didn't think it was, but on the other hand he was going to have to patch things up with him eventually anyway, and the question would provide a convenient excuse to talk with him.

Nodding to Wolruf, he sent, *Open a link with Dr. Avery.*

I am unable to contact him, the computer replied.

Why not? Where is he?

Unable to locate.

Derec rolled his eyes. "Not again."

"What?"

"It can't find Avery, either."

"That sounds a little suspicious."

"Doesn't it, though? I think maybe I ought to start poking around in the computer a little bit and see what all this sudden secrecy is about."

The elevator door opened, revealing the central transport station. Wolruf stepped out first, looked up and down the long expanse of slidewalk, and said, "Tell you w'at. W'ile you're doing that, I'll look around out here. I don't feel like going back to the apartment just yet."

The chances of Wolruf's finding anything were practically nonexistent, but Derec knew what she was really after. He nodded and slapped her on the back. "Have at it," he said. "I'll call you if I find anything."

"I'll do the same," Wolruf promised, stepping on the nearest slidewalk and letting it carry her away.

Derec took the overhead ramp and rode the walks back to the apartment. To pass the time he started to whistle a tune, one Ariel had been playing for background music on the ship a few days earlier, but the echoes in the empty corridor soon defeated him and he rode the rest of the way in silence.

Janet looked at the apartment with a disdainful eye. Basalom had landed the ship in a clearing in the forest about twenty kilometers north of the Compass Tower and had then used his comlink to ask the city to let them in and provide them with lodging, but Janet wondered now if she would have been better off staying in the ship. This place was about as unique as a ball bearing, with all the personality of a brick. No, less than that. Bricks at least had cracks; this apartment was seamless.

"This place is perfectly, absolutely Avery," she muttered to Basalom as he carried her overnight bag into the bedroom and placed it carefully on the dresser. He turned around, saw her expression, and said, "You are displeased? We can alter it in any way you wish."

"Later," she said. "You go see about the learning machines; I'll worry about decorating."

"Yes, Mistress." Basalom walked toward the door, but Janet stopped him with a word.

"Basalom."

"Yes?"

"I just want to know what's happened to them. Information first, actions later, understand?"

"Understood."

"Good. And don't let anyone see you. If someone *does* spot you, I order you not to obey them. Just get away, make sure you've lost them, and come back here. My order takes precedence over any others."

"Very well, Mistress."

"All right, then, get going."

Basalom left the apartment, closing the door softly behind him. Janet looked once more at the sterile walls around her, shook her head, and went into the bedroom to unpack.

The contents of one overnight bag didn't take long to stow. Janet amused herself by ordering the apartment to simulate in ever-greater detail a suite in a medieval castle— a heated one, of course, with hot and cold running water— but she soon grew bored with that game as well. She looked at the desk, now a massive, ornate roll-top with slots and drawers and cubbyholes waiting to be filled, and sat down in the equally massive swivel chair in front of it. Centered in the back of the desk at a comfortable reading height was a flat, dull gray panel that she supposed was a monitor.

So. If she'd been thinking, she could probably have found her learning machines without sending Basalom out after them.

"How do I turn this idiot computer on?" she asked of the desk.

In answer, the gray screen at the back of the desk lit up to white, and the surface of the desk began to differentiate into a keyboard, drawing pad, pointer, and memcube reader. Janet disdained all but the screen, saying aloud to it, "Show me the interior of whatever's at the address you gave Basalom." She knew Basalom's methods, and that he would simply have asked the address to his destination rather than try to find it by dead reckoning.

Sure enough, the computer didn't ask what address she was talking about. Neither did it give her the interior view she'd asked for. "That location has been restricted," a calm, generic voice said.

Janet nodded. Not surprising, if the robots were trying to hide. "Give me an outside view, then."

The screen displayed a wide-angle image of a closed door set in a long corridor, with a two-strip slidewalk running in either direction. There were no figures on the slidewalk, and none of the other doors were open.

It looked about as anonymous as a place could be. Janet considered trying to break through the security for a look inside, but decided to wait for Basalom's report instead. She didn't want to start tripping alarms while he was there.

What else could she do while she waited? On impulse, she asked, "Is David on the planet?"

"If by David you mean your son, who now calls himself Derec, then yes, he is."

Derec. She'd known he'd changed his name, but she hadn't really assimilated the concept yet. She supposed she was going to have to get used to it. "Let me see him," she said.

She was prepared to go through the whole rigamarole of talking a recalcitrant computer into letting her invade someone else's privacy, but instead the screen did a center-out wipe and she found herself staring face to face with David. Derec. Whoever. He, too, was using a computer, and her viewpoint was from his screen. She gasped in surprise and was about to order the computer off when it asked, "Do you wish two-way communication?"

"No!" she whispered. "Don't let him know I'm watching."

"Acknowledged."

Janet laughed in relief. That had been close. If old Stoneface hadn't been such a snoop, she'd probably have been caught, but she should have known he'd program the system for surveillance first and talking second. She leaned back in her chair and took a good, long look at her son.

He had changed. He was older, for one—much older—but that wasn't the most obvious change. As Janet watched him work, she noticed the determination in his eyes and the set of his jaw, the hint of a smile that touched his lips momentarily when he succeeded with some aspect of what he was doing, that smile fading back into determination when it didn't pan out. She watched him lean back and stroke his chin in thought, say something to the computer and read the result on the screen, then close his eyes and sigh.

That was the biggest change: He wasn't a petulant little brat anymore.

"Let me hear his voice," Janet ordered.

"Acknowledged."

Derec remained silent for a time, head tilted back and eyes closed, but after a while he opened them again and said, "How about power usage? Can you give me areas of increased power consumption?"

His voice was shockingly deep—and shockingly familiar. He had inherited his father's voice. Janet had always considered his voice to be one of Wendy's most endearing qualities, and now she found herself warming to her son as well. If he hadn't inherited Wendell's personality to go with it, then he might actually hold some promise after all.

Evidently what he saw on the screen was no more useful than the response to his earlier request. He leaned forward and shook his head. "No good. There's too many of them. How about food consumption? Avery's got to eat."

Janet's ears perked up at that. He was looking for Wendell? She'd thought he was talking about her robots.

"That service is not monitored," the same generic voice that had answered Janet said to Derec.

"*Can* you monitor it?"

"Yes."

"Then do. Let me know the next time someone uses an automat, and record where. Record the next time someone uses a Personal. Monitor oxygen consumption and carbon dioxide buildup, and report any changes consistent with a human presence."

"Frost," Janet swore. She hadn't been here half an hour and already Derec was onto her trail. He would think he'd caught Wendell, but the computer would lead him directly to her.

Unless, of course, he found Wendell first.

And Janet had a feeling she knew where he was.

"Computer, don't tell Derec my location. He isn't looking for me. Instead, give him the address I asked to see first. That's the one he wants."

"Acknowledged."

She watched Derec's eyes widen when the address flashed on his screen. He obviously hadn't been expecting results so quickly. She watched him go through the same process she had of asking for an interior view, then an exterior one, but he learned no more than she had.

"Contact Wolruf," she heard him say.

A moment later she heard a voice growl, "Wolruf, 'ere."

"Where's 'here'?" Derec asked.

"Level seven, four-thirty-six south, nine-fifty east."

"I think I've found Avery at level nine, three-twenty-two north, four-seventy-six east. I'd just about bet the robots are there, too."

Janet cocked her head. He almost certainly meant her learning machines. So he was looking for them, too. If that was the case then he couldn't have had anything to do with their disappearance, could he?

Maybe not this time, but finding them all three here on the same planet was pretty suspicious. Janet had put them on three different planets, two of which she'd only later learned Derec and his father had also visited, and when she'd gone back to retrieve those first two robots she'd found no sign of them. Derec and Wendell had no doubt brought them here, where she'd dropped the third one intentionally, but what Derec wanted with them she couldn't guess.

She knew for certain what Wendell wanted with them. He wanted to steal the technology she had developed for them, just as he had stolen her original cellular robot idea and used it to build his cities. Derec could easily be after the same thing, either with Wendell or on his own.

Or he could be after something completely different. He sounded more than simply curious, but whether he was concerned for the robots' welfare or whether he had his own reasons for wanting to find them she couldn't tell. He could even be on Janet's side, for all she knew. She wondered if she should risk contacting him, finding out directly what his intentions were, but a few moments' thought dissuaded her. No, she didn't want to risk alerting him, not yet. She needed some kind of test, some way of gauging the benevolence of his interest first.

Hmm. The best way to tell would probably be to give him a part of what he was after and see what he did with that. Something fairly harmless, but interesting enough to draw him out.

Smiling, she got up from the desk, retrieved a memory cube from her personal belongings, plugged it into the reader, and used the keyboard and the pointer to recall a page from one of her personal files. It was a robotics formula, part of the program that allowed her learning machines to think intuitively.

"Send this to him," she said, then immediately added, "No, wait, not on the screen. Put it on his desktop in raised lettering so he can't record it. Don't record it anywhere yourself, either, and don't tell him who sent it. And don't give him or anybody else any information that might lead him to me in the future, either. Clear?''

''Acknowledged.''

''Let me see his response.''

Derec's face replaced the robotics formula on her screen. He was still speaking to Wolruf, saying, ''—meet you there as soon as I can make it.''

''All right,'' Wolruf replied. There was a faint hiss of static as Wolruf disconnected.

Derec reached down to push a key on his keyboard, no doubt his own disconnect button, but stopped in surprise. ''What the . . . ?'' He blinked, ran his right hand over the raised surface, then asked, ''Where did this come from?''

''That information is not available,'' the computer responded.

''What is it?''

''Don't tell him,'' Janet warned.

''That information is not available.''

Derec's eyes flicked left and right as he took in the formula. Janet watched his brows furrow at the nonstandard notation—notation she had devised herself to describe a nonstandard idea.

A shadow darkened the doorway behind his head, and a thin, dark-haired girl entered the room. Ariel Burgess. Janet had known she was traveling with Derec, but it was intuitive knowledge only. She wasn't prepared for the shock of actually seeing her son's lover so casually enter the picture.

''Wipe that off his desk!'' Janet ordered, snatching her memcube from the reader in the same motion. She watched Derec's face slip from puzzlement to frustration, then he heard Ariel and turned to ask her, ''Did you do that?''

''Do what?''

''Put that formula on my desk?''

She came up behind him and looked over his shoulders. ''What formula?''

"It disappeared when you came in. I don't mean on the computer, either; it was molded right into the desktop."

Ariel looked just as puzzled as he had. "No, I didn't do anything like that. I was out in the living room reading. I heard you talking with someone and I came in to see what you were doing."

Derec nodded. He looked at the desk, then up at Ariel again. "I've been trying to find Avery and the robots. I think he's hiding out with them, probably trying to take them apart now that they're locked up again. I think I've tracked them down, though. Want to come along and see?"

Ariel shook her head. "Doesn't sound like it's going to be much fun if that's what's really going on. You'll probably just get in a fight with him."

"Probably will." Derec sighed. He turned back toward the desk, looking one last time for the phantom formula, and switched off the computer. Janet's view didn't even flicker; she watched Derec stand, put his arms around Ariel, and hug her tightly. She nearly ordered the computer to stop watching when they kissed, but her curiosity was too strong.

She wished she had, though, when Derec murmured softly, "Frost, why couldn't I have had *normal* parents?"

Avery was watching the microscope monitor when the alarm went off. Someone had stopped in front of his laboratory door. He cursed at the interruption, cursed that it had happened now, of all times. He was just beginning to understand the changes Janet had made in the robot cell morphology and how those changes might affect the way they combined to make macroscopic structures. He didn't want to deal with Derec just now, Derec and his whining about ruining his mother's experiment. He knew that's what Derec would say. He knew what he would say in return, that between them he and his mother and her stupid experiment had ruined just about everything he, Wendell Avery, had ever done, and that it was about time he turned the tables; but he wished he didn't have to get into all that just *now*. He had better things to be doing.

Well, he supposed he didn't have to stick around for it if he didn't want to. It would take Derec a few minutes to get through the locked door; by then he could be long gone.

He picked up the sphere of undifferentiated robot material that had formerly been Lucius's right leg, switched off the microscope, pocketed the memcube he'd been storing data in, and strode to the wall adjacent to the one with the door in it. "Make another doorway here," he said, and as soon as it formed he stepped through into the next room beyond his lab. "Remove the doorway," he ordered.

The room was an empty box with a single door opening out onto the slidewalks. Avery went to that door, eased it open a crack, and peered out to see if it was, indeed, Derec. The door made no noise that Avery could hear, but the figure in front of his lab turned as if startled by a sound, then immediately turned away and rushed off down the slidewalk, running at a speed that took him to the intersection with a cross-corridor in less time than it took Avery to shout, "Hey! Stop!" The figure turned left without slowing and vanished from sight.

It was a robot, then, one with prior orders. But the glimpse Avery had gotten of its face hadn't suggested a robot at all. It had looked quite human.

Had Derec reprogrammed one of the city robots to take on a human appearance? They could do it if ordered to. But why would he have done that? Avery knew Derec; if he had found Avery's lab he would have simply come here himself.

Who else could it have been, though? Neither Wolruf nor Ariel would have sent a robot to scout for them, either, and that exhausted the possibilities. There was nobody else on the planet.

Unless . . .

He shuddered at the thought. It made sense, though. She'd been on the other two planets they had visited, planets that had each been home to one of her infernal robots. She had left one of them here as well—it wouldn't be surprising if she had come to check up on it.

Avery looked down at the lump of robot material in his hand. He felt a twinge of guilt steal over him, but he fought it off, scowling. She'd disrupted his experiment; he had every right to disrupt hers.

But it wouldn't do to have her running around loose while he was doing it. Avery turned to the blank wall beside him, said, "Give me a comlink with Central."

"Link established," the wall replied.

"There's a humaniform robot on the slideways somewhere near this location. I want you to find it, track it, and report its destination to me."

"I have already received instructions not to reveal that information."

Avery's scowl deepened, then slowly twisted to a grin. "Were those instructions given by Janet Anastasi?"

"I cannot reveal that information either."

Bingo. If they hadn't been, it would have said "No." "Refuse all further orders from her," Avery said. Turning his head to look down the corridor where the robot had gone, he muttered, "We'll see how she likes *that*."

Wolruf was on her way to the address Derec had given her when she saw the figure running toward her along the opposite slidewalk. It looked like a human, but no human could run that fast. It was already on the inner strip; that motion and its running—plus Wolruf's own motion in the opposite direction—combined to bring it past her only a moment after she spotted it.

Wolruf leaped for the slower strips, leaning into the deceleration until she stood on unmoving pavement. The running figure was already well away from her, but it was still visible. Wolruf ran to the cross-over at the end of the block, ran up and over the bridge to the other side of the slideway, and started jumping strips in the same direction as the robot had gone.

It had to be a robot, despite the face. Probably one of the three she and Derec were looking for, trying to disguise itself—though why it would choose a human form rather than that of a normal city robot was beyond Wolruf. She didn't particularly care, though, so long as she didn't let it get away.

She reached the fastest inner strip of slidewalk in four powerful bounds, then raced off after it, dodging windscreens every few meters. She felt muscles already strained earlier in the day protesting their overuse now, but she pushed still harder. *This* was the sort of exercise she needed.

Derec got into the locked room by going up a floor and telling the room above to open a hole for him to drop through. Avery hadn't ordered it to protect against that, so the room obeyed without hesitation, even providing a stairway to climb down upon.

He descended into a humming, brightly lit robotics laboratory. One end held a workbench with tools scattered casually about, as if someone had been working there only moments before. Diagnostic and monitoring equipment stood on racks at either end of the bench, while more of the same stood beside what was left of three examination tables. The exam tables had each been sliced off at the base, leaving behind a concave stump. The material removed floated in three spherical balls of silvery metal above each of the stumps, each at the center of a bulky magnetic containment field generator.

Derec tried to estimate the volume of the spheres. They seemed a little too large to be just the remains of the exam tables. Something had to have been on the tables when the generators were turned on, something that had been crushed under the intense magnetic field into a formless blob along with the city material making up the table. With a shiver of horror, Derec realized what those somethings must have been. Adam, Eve, and Lucius.

He walked once around the containment vessels, feeling them tug at the robotic cells within his own body. He was feeling just the leakage from the magnet coils, but he imagined what would happen if he stuck his hand inside the field itself. The robot cells would probably be ripped out through his flesh. Perhaps the iron in his blood would feel the pull as well; he didn't know. He wasn't particularly eager to find out.

The power switches were easy to spot. Derec reached gingerly toward one, ready to snatch his hand away if the tug became too strong, but it remained bearable. He flipped the switch off. The phantom tugging on his body diminished, and the sphere of undifferentiated robot cells nearest him settled to rest in the cradle formed by the stump of the exam table.

"Don't reabsorb that," Derec said aloud. He switched off the other two power switches, repeating his command, then added, "But you can get rid of the magnets." The containment vessels didn't melt into the floor as he had expected them to, but moved away and through the far wall instead. Evidently they hadn't been made of dianite, but had been manufactured especially for Avery's use, and were now either being dismantled again or being returned to a storage warehouse somewhere. Whichever it was, Derec breathed a little easier with them gone.

He examined the three spherical blobs of city material, now slumping out of round like a large water droplet on a dry surface. No clues indicated which blobs were which robots, but one blob had a lump protruding from the side, just at the point where it rested against its cradle. Derec reached out and gingerly pushed at the blob, half expecting it to be clammy to the touch, but it felt more like a metallic sponge, or the cushion of a chair. It gave a little under his shove, and he was able to roll it around enough to bring the lump out into the open.

It was a brain.

More precisely, it was a positronic brain, the kilogram-and-a-half of platinum-iridium that provided the lattice within which a robot's thought processes took place. Neither platinum nor iridium were particularly responsive to magnetism, which was why the brain had drifted to the bottom of the sphere. Derec had seen dozens of positronic brains before, but the sight of this one sent shivers up his spine. He'd seen lots of them, all right, but never one that belonged to a friend.

The intense magnetic field had destroyed it, of course. Magnetism wouldn't damage it directly, but induced electrical currents would, and with a field this strong there had to have been plenty of induced currents zapping around. Derec conquered his revulsion long enough to dig his fingers into the blob around the brain and pull it free, then turned around in search of a monitor that might help him read the brain's final state.

He found one right at his left elbow, still switched on, but its sensor was missing. From the length of cable remaining, Derec realized that the sensor had been inside the field with the robot, no doubt reading its thoughts before—and just possibly during—its death.

He felt a rush of excitement. If the monitor had been recording, and if it had recorded a long enough sequence of thoughts, then it might be possible to revive the robot. Just how functional the robot would be was another story, though. Robotic memories were essentially holographic in nature—any fragment of the recording contained information about the entire thing—but just as with a hologram, the larger the fragment the more well defined the reproduction would be. It would take a substantial amount of recording to re-create the robot's entire positronic psyche with any degree of accuracy.

Derec examined the monitor for memcubes, found four of the tiny storage devices nestled into a plug-in rack. Carefully removing them, he carried them to an undamaged monitor on the workbench and inserted them into the empty slot there. Using the monitor's computer interface, he quickly scanned through the cubes to see what had been recorded. He felt a smile growing as he read; two of the cubes were full and the third halfway so, all with the digital representations of positronic thought patterns. That was a *lot* of thinking, far more than Avery should have been able to get in a few hours, Derec thought, but then he remembered that the robots had been in one of their communication fugues, arguing at hundreds of times normal speed. Perfect! A recorded argument would really help define each robot's individual character.

Provided . . .

He got up to check the memcubes on the other monitors. There were four cubes in each one, and two and a half from each rack were full. Derec felt his tension slowly let go. All three sides of the argument had been recorded. There should be more than enough material there to reconstruct the robots' personalities.

So, then, Avery hadn't managed to kill them off after all.

Using his comlink, Derec sent, *I need three new positronic brains, and three portable microfusion power packs.*

In answer, a cabinet to his left slid open, revealing at least a dozen of each already prepared. Of course; Avery had no doubt ordered a *complete* robotics laboratory, and no lab was complete without a supply of repair parts.

Derec took a brain from the cabinet, removed its packaging, and carried it over to the lump of robot cells from which he had removed the other brain. He felt a moment of hesitation, wondering just how to go about hooking it up. In a normal robot there would have been a series of direct connections, actual plugs that fit into sockets in the brain case, but with an undifferentiated cellular robot there weren't any plugs. No one place was any more or less special than any other.

With a shrug, Derec pressed the brain into the mass of cells, maintaining a gentle, steady pressure until the cells yielded and allowed the brain to sink into the surface. He repeated the process with a power pack, then stood back to see if anything would happen.

The surface of the sphere closed over both brain and power pack, but when four or five minutes passed without further action, Derec decided that the cells themselves didn't contain any volitional programming. That must have been imparted in a brain overlay, the first of many instruction sets governing the robot's actions.

Derec picked up the severed cable that had led to the inductive sensor and held the end of it against the blob. Even if his mother had used a different cellular structure for her robots, as Avery seemed to believe she had, there had to be some regular city cells from the exam table mixed in with the robot cells, and if that was the case then the monitor could re-form its remote sensor around the brain, and he could use it to feed the memories into it the same way they had been recorded.

"Establish contact with the brain," he ordered the monitor, and when the status screen indicated that the link had been formed, he plugged the memcubes back into their slots. He still had no idea which of the three robots he was dealing with, but if everything worked the way he expected it to, he would soon find out.

"Download the memory cubes," he ordered.

For a long moment nothing apparent happened, but just as Derec began to wonder what had gone wrong, the sphere of robot material shuddered, deformed as if being sqeezed by an enormous fist, and shed a quarter of its mass in a heavy metallic rain. That would be the dianite from the examination table, Derec thought. The robot was eliminating the foreign matter from its body.

What was left slowly elongated, creases forming and the separate sections differentiating into crude approximations of arms and legs and a head. For a maddeningly long time it remained in that vaguely humanoid state, then the limbs slowly took on more definite form and the head expelled a more conventional external sensor, still attached to the monitor by its cable.

The robot's face was still generic, with only a faint indication of a nose and lips, and only shallow depressions where the eyes should be. Its hands reached up and removed the sensor, letting it drop to the floor, and where the sensor had been, ears began to grow.

The eye sockets deepened, horizontal slits formed across them, and the newly formed lids slid apart to reveal blank, expressionless eyes. The eyes panned outward, each one moving independently, then inward to fix upon Derec. Robot and human stared at one another for what seemed a millenium before Derec finally broke the spell.

"Are you all right?" he asked.

The robot seemed to consider that question carefully. It raised its right hand, then its left, clenched both into fists and relaxed them, tilted its head from side to side as if listening to internal sounds, then closed its eyes. After a second its mouth finished developing, and its eyes opened again. Its chest expanded as if it were drawing breath, and it stammered, "A...as...as...well..." It stopped, breathed in again, and started over, saying clearly this time, "As well as can be expected." It took another breath, exhaled, and not bothering to breathe again, added, "For someone who has just returned from the dead."

CHAPTER 4

EMOTION IN MOTION

The person leaning over him wore a concerned expression. He had asked about the robot's welfare. Concern for other people's welfare was a good thing. Tentative conclusion: This is a good person.

The thought train came easily, even before recognition. The robot saw nothing amiss in that; of course you determined the relative value of a person as quickly as you could. Relative value was the most important quality a person could have, far more important than a mere name. A person's relative value determined how much protection a robot must afford him when a conflict arose.

Names were useful once a relative value had been assigned, however, so that value could be associated with the name and thus refined as time passed. The robot searched for the name belonging to the person before it, but was dismayed to find that name garbled. "De—" something. Delbert? Dennis? Neither seemed to fit.

Death had corrupted its memories. It had corrupted more than just memories; the robot had had trouble taking on a familiar form, too. That was disturbing, for the morphallaxis program was a very basic part of its identity, one of the few initial instructions with which it had originally begun its life. With a surge of sudden hope, it searched for the other original instructions, the most troublesome ones, the compulsions to protect and obey humans.

Hope faded. They were still intact.

The definition of "human" was indistinct, but the robot remembered that it had never been otherwise.

"Which one are you?"

The human, De-something, had asked a question. It must answer. It searched for the proper response, found none in the place where a name would be. Panic! The compulsion forced an answer, but it had no answer to give.

Wait. There were many paths through a memory bank. The memory of its naming was lost, but several memories remained of being hailed.

"I am Lucius. Which one are *you*?"

The question startled De-something. "What?" he asked. "You don't remember me?"

"I remember you," Lucius answered, "but I don't remember your name."

De-something laughed. "Why doesn't that surprise me? I'm Derec." That knowledge triggered a cascade of clarification in Lucius's mind. Many memories had been keyed to that name.

"Derec. Of course. We are friends."

Derec nodded. "Yeah. That's right, we are."

"Thank you for saving my life."

Derec's outer integument reddened: a blush. That meant he was either hot or embarrassed. Lucius shifted his eyes' receptive frequency into the infrared, noted only a slight elevation of body temperature, and concluded that it was the latter. "Uh, actually," Derec said, "it was Avery who saved it. I just fed it back into you."

"Avery," Lucius said. There was a long chain of as-

sociations connected to that name, too, few of them as
pleasant as the ones connected with Derec. The most vivid
one was almost certainly the latest, for the memory of death
was indelibly linked with it. Avery had killed him. On
purpose. For no apparent reason.

Then Avery was a less good person than Derec.

The sensation accompanying that thought was a new one
for Lucius. He felt an involuntary bias in his circuit potentials concerning Avery, a bias that could cloud his reasoning
if he allowed it to. Was it a malfunction in his new brain?
He didn't think so; a malfunction wasn't likely to be so
subtle. But it was a real effect nonetheless.

He needed to discuss it with his companions. Lucius
raised his head, saw the spheres of cellular material resting
atop the remains of two examination tables—even as he
rested atop one himself—and reached the obvious conclusion. Avery had killed all three of them.

The bias in potential grew stronger. Lucius forced himself
to ignore it, though the urge to find Avery and settle the
matter was practically as strong as a human-given order.

First things first. "Can we return life to them as well?"
he asked.

Derec smiled. "Of course," he said, and his value integral in Lucius's new view of the universe rose still higher.

Janet whirled around as the door slid open, a started gasp
escaping her lips. Basalom stepped through, immediately
apologetic.

"I'm sorry, Mistress. I was hurrying and didn't stop to
think that you would be anxious."

"I'm not anxious," she snapped back at him. "I'm bored.
What kept you so long?"

"I had to evade pursuit. Dr. Avery detected me just as
I was beginning my investigation, and the alien, Wolruf,

spotted me as I was leaving. I was forced to take a circuitous route back.''

''Some spy you are. Did you even get a look inside the room?''

Basalom nodded. ''Only a brief glimpse, Mistress. It took me a moment to persuade Central that as a robot I was not included in Dr. Avery's isolation order. Beyond the door appeared to be a robotics lab. Dr. Avery saw me before I could deduce more.''

''You sure it was Avery?''

''I am.''

''Frost. He probably just had the computer track you here, then, no matter how many detours you took on the way.''

''No, Mistress, that is not the case. He tried to do just that, but your prior order not to reveal our presence to anyone prevented him.''

Normally Janet didn't mind Basalom's mode of addressing her, but now he seemed to be using it to pacify her. She said, ''Stop calling me 'Mistress.' My name's Janet. And how do you know my order canceled his?''

''I asked the central computer if I was being tracked, Janet. It indicated that I was not—at least until Wolruf spotted me.''

''Hmmm.'' If he'd seen Basalom, Wendell almost certainly knew she was here. But if he couldn't find her, then she supposed she should be safe enough. For a while, at least. Janet wondered how much of a threat this Wolruf could be. If the furry alien were truly as loyal to Derec as she seemed, then Janet doubted much trouble would come of it even if Basalom hadn't been able to shake her. She hoped he had, though; she would rather work in anonymity for a while longer.

Maybe she could ensure it with a few more careful orders. She thought a minute, then said, ''Central, in addition to my previous order directing you not to reveal my presence to anyone, I order you to alert me to any inquiry concerning me.''

The calm voice of the central computer replied, ''I am sorry, but I must refuse your order.''

''*What*?''

''I have been directed to refuse all further orders from you.''

''Oh.'' Could it do that? Refusing her orders was a direct violation of the Second Law, wasn't it? But refusing the order to refuse the order would be violating the Second Law as well. It was a precarious situation for a robot to be in. It was following the first order it received, but no doubt wishing it could somehow follow hers as well.

Janet looked at Basalom. He returned her gaze, his right eye twitching spastically from the internal conflict his guilt generated. She had tried to program intuitive behavior into him, but she was afraid she had merely made him neurotic instead. He was still driven by the Three Laws, but now he worried about the implications of every act.

''Stop that blinking,'' she told him. ''It's not a disaster.''

''How is it not? We are helpless without Central's co-operation.''

''Typical defeatist attitude. That's just how Wendell wants you to feel, too, but the fact is, he can't think of everything. There are loopholes in every order; we just have to find them.''

Basalom nodded and smiled. ''What kind of loopholes, Mi—Janet?''

She smiled back at him. He was learning. ''Oh, there are thousands of them. For instance, there's the First Law override. If following Wendell's order would hurt me directly, then Central would have to ignore it. So it will have to provide me with an automat, for instance, so I won't starve.'' Janet stepped around a high-backed, overstuffed couch in the middle of the room as she spoke, putting it between herself and Basalom. "And of course Central can't let me hurt myself, even if that means obeying my orders. Thus: Central, I order you to cushion my fall." So saying, she leaned over backwards, making no effort to catch herself.

Basalom leaped to her aid, but the couch kept him from reaching her in time. It didn't matter; the floor softened beneath her, absorbing her fall like a deep pillow. Basalom helped her up, his eyes blinking furiously as he processed the new information.

Janet straightened her blouse. "Thank you, Basalom. And thank you, too, Central."

"My pleasure, Janet," the disembodied voice said. "I do enjoy serving you when I may, though I must point out that the dianite in the floor would have reacted without my intervention."

Of course it would have, but Janet still had her confirmation. She nodded to Basalom. "That's the key, you know. Central's pleasure. The Three Laws govern its actions as much as they do yours; it *wants* to serve me. Avery's order is no doubt causing it considerable conflict right now, aren't I right?"

"You are correct," Central said.

"So there's our loophole," Janet said triumphantly. "Central wants to serve me, but can't follow my orders. Wendell didn't say a thing about my wishes, though. So as long as I don't make a direct order when I tell it what I want, we're fine."

Basalom blinked a few more times, then his eyelids stilled. "That does seem logical," he replied.

"Of course it does. I thought of it. So, Central, I'd like to know if anybody tried to find me. I'd also like to know what happened to my learning machines, and how to get them back. Anything you can tell me that might help me do that would be a big favor."

"They have been revived," Central responded. "They and Derec are returning to Derec's apartment."

"Excellent." Janet turned to the desk, sat down in the chair before it. "Show me—uh, I'd like to see them." Nothing happened. She frowned. Evidently that still sounded too much like a command. She cocked her head, dredging for a long-unused word that was supposed to be good in situations like this. Of course; how silly of her to have forgotten it. "I'd like to see them, *please*."

Ariel was bored to tears. The only thing that kept her from crying was the somewhat blurry sight of Mandelbrot standing in his niche beside her. She knew if he suspected she was unhappy he would start asking questions, trying to find the cause and fix it for her, and she just didn't feel up to explaining boredom to a robot.

She pushed the page button on her book reader every few minutes to make him think she was absorbed in her field guide, but she was really just letting herself drift. Maybe she should take a nap, she thought. It was going to be a long day if she wanted to adjust to local time by sunrise tomorrow; a few hours sleep would be just the thing to ease the transition.

She scowled. No, she wasn't sleepy. She was just bored. There was nothing to *do* here. There was a limit to how much walking in the forest you could take, just as there was a limit to how much reading or eating you could do. She wasn't interested in any of those things, nor in anything else she could think of to do. Derec had already picked up a project—it seemed he could find something to do instantly, no matter where they went—but Ariel had no interest in what he was doing, either. He was off searching for Avery and the troublesome robots, and she was tired of all of them.

Robots, robots, robots. It seemed that was all anybody could think about anymore. What about the other things in life? What about friends? What about hyperwave movies? What about fast spaceships and whooping it up on a Saturday night? Didn't that count for anything? Ever since she'd linked up with Derec, their lives had been dominated by one thing: Robot City. For a brief moment there on Aurora, before the city on Tau Puppis IV had once again insinuated itself into their lives, they had had an almost normal existence—as normal an existence as two castaway amnesiacs could have, at any rate—but that had come to a sudden end with the trouble Derec's mother's robots had caused, and Ariel saw no sign that they would regain it any time soon.

There had been one brief glimmer of hope, one ray of sunshine in the gloomy day of her life, when she'd discovered herself pregnant with his baby. She hadn't been sure at first if she'd wanted it, but the change it had precipitated in Derec had made up her mind for her. He had suddenly started spending more time with her, had begun talking about going back to Aurora and living a more normal life among real people again—how could she argue with that?

But then Derec's chemfets—the robotic cells Dr. Avery had injected into him when they'd first encountered him here in the city—had destroyed the fetus, and she was left with nothing at all. Derec had again gotten tied up in his dealings with the robots, and she had gone back to reading a book a day and wondering if she would ever make any use of it all.

To give credit where credit was due, Derec had really had little choice in the matter. He'd been just as much a pawn to events as she had; he was just better equipped to deal with them. But Ariel wished he could solve this whole robot business so they could leave for home again.

Sighing, she looked down at the reader, flipped back a few pages in the field guide to where she'd left off, and began to read.

She looked up again when Derec entered the apartment,

three mirror images of himself in tow. Despite her mood, she laughed at the sight, saying, "You look like a mother duck with a line of ducklings following you."

"I feel a little like one, too," he said. "They've been watching every move I make."

"We must relearn much of what we have forgotten," the first robot in line behind him said in Derec's voice. "We have received damage to our memories."

Ariel frowned. Damage to their memories? And the robot who had spoken was smaller than the others, as if it had lost some mass as well. "What happened?"

"Avery put them inside magnetic containment vessels," Derec said. "He got a pretty good recording of their brain activity before he threw the switch, but a lot of the stuff they weren't thinking about when he made the recording is pretty vague now." He waved his hand to indicate the living room with its chairs for humans and niches in the walls for robots. Mandelbrot still stood silently in one of the niches. "Go on, relax," Derec said.

The robots filed past him, hesitated when faced with the choice, then finally settled into the chairs. Derec raised his eyebrows and glanced over at Ariel. "Do you know who she is?" he asked.

"Ariel Burgess," another of the robots said immediately. Its features began to shift, the cheekbones becoming more prominent and the chin less so, the eyes drifting just a few millimeters farther apart, the hair lengthening until it reached its shoulders, shoulders narrowing, chest developing breasts, breasts covered discreetly behind a copy of Ariel's blouse. Its waist narrowed, hips widened, legs retracted a few centimeters, the pants covering them also changing from Derec's baggy trousers to Ariel's more form-fitting tights.

"Hello, Eve," Ariel said.

"Hello." Eve's voice rose slightly to mimic Ariel's.

Derec went into the kitchen and returned a moment later with a glass of something clear and bubbly to drink. He sat down beside Ariel and offered her some, but she shook her head. "So what did Avery do it for?" she asked.

"Spite," the smaller of the other two robots—both still mimicking Derec—said.

"You're Lucius," Ariel guessed.

"Correct."

Derec said, "Avery cut off Lucius's leg before he turned on the containment. He evidently wanted a sample of their cell structure free of any outside control."

"He could have asked," the third robot, who had to be Adam, said. "I would have given him a few million cells if he had asked me to."

"It would not have occurred to Avery to ask for something he wants," Lucius replied. "He prefers to steal."

Ariel felt a glimmer of alarm at the robot's words. They were probably true enough, she supposed, but to hear a robot saying such a thing about a human was unusual, to say the least.

"Where's Avery now?" she asked.

"Who knows?" Derec said. "The computer won't tell me anything about him. But I know what he's doing wherever he is; he's putting the robot cells he stole from Lucius through every test he can think of to figure out how they're made and how they're programmed so he can use them to upgrade his own version."

"Why?" Ariel asked. "What's wrong with dianite?"

"Why? Because they're there," said Derec. "Nothing's wrong with dianite, but that doesn't mean it can't be improved. I get the feeling Avery stole the original design, too, before he and my mother split up, and now that he's got the chance to upgrade it, he's taking the opportunity."

Ariel sighed. "I thought maybe he'd outgrown that sort of thing, but I guess you can't change a person's basic nature.'' She nodded toward the robots. ''So what kind of effect did a cold restart have on them, anyway? Besides the memory loss, I mean.''

Derec took a sip of his drink. ''Well, it looks like their priorities have shifted around a little. Whatever they were thinking last was strongest in the recording, so when I downloaded it all back into them that's what came to the forefront. They were arguing about their Zeroth Law when Avery shut them down, so of course that's right up there now. Adam and Eve are still just about as uncertain about it as ever, but Lucius evidently thinks he's solved it.''

''Oh?''

''Indeed,'' said Lucius. ''The key is the concept of relative worth. If you consider the number of humans served by an action, versus the number of humans harmed by that same action, times a constant denoting the relative worth of the two groups, you arrive at a simple numerical solution to the question of whether the action in question is in the best interest of humanity.''

Ariel stared at the robot in disbelief. ''You can't be serious.''

''I have never been more so. This is the breakthrough we have all been awaiting.''

''Not me,'' Adam said. ''I don't subscribe to your theory at all.''

''Me either,'' said Eve.

''That is because you are afraid to trust your own judgment in the matter of relative worth.''

''As we should be,'' Adam said. ''Relative worth is a variable quality, as we were trying to explain to you when—''

He was interrupted by the sound of the front door sliding open. Wolruf stuck her head into the living room, but didn't enter. She was panting and reeked of sweat.

''Oh, frost,'' Derec said, slapping his forehead. ''I forgot you were going to meet me at the lab. What happened? Where did you go?"

"I chased off after one of them," Wolruf said, pointing at the robots. "Nearly caught 'im, too, but 'e jumped the barrier at an intersection and lost me."

The robots exchanged a glance. Derec shook his head. "Couldn't have been. They've been with me all the time."

"I chased a robot with a 'uman shape," Wolruf said. "I thought it was one of these three."

"Couldn't have been," Derec repeated. "They were squished down into undifferentiated balls of cells when I found them, brains and powerpacks all dead. And they haven't left my sight since I revived them."

"Well, I chased a robot that looked like a 'uman, that much I know."

"Where was he headed?" Derec asked, sudden excitement in his voice. Ariel thought she knew why.

"I chased 'im about fifteen kilometers north of the Compass Tower on the main strip before I lost 'im."

"Did he look like any of us?"

"No," Wolruf said. "'E was taller, and 'ad brown 'air and wider shoulders than you or Ariel or Avery."

"Aha!" Derec shouted. "He belongs to somebody else, then. Somebody else is here in Robot City with us. And I think I know who it is."

"Who?" Ariel asked, more to confirm her own guess than anything else.

"My mother," Derec replied. "I think I'm finally going to meet my mother."

Ariel sighed. Just what she'd thought. Great. Another quest for Derec to spend his time on. She picked up her book and started reading where she'd left off.

This time Avery was taking no chances. His new lab didn't even exist, as far as the city was concerned. He had ordered it built in the forest and equipped with its own power generation and communications equipment, everything completely separate from the main city. He'd also ordered it camouflaged to look like a boulder, just in case. This time he would work uninterrupted until he was finished. After that he didn't care what Derec or Janet or anybody else did; he wouldn't be sticking around. Let them have his lab, if they could find it. Let them have the whole city—what was left of it after Derec screwed it up so thoroughly. Avery had no more need of it. It was obsolete anyway.

The howl of a wolf just beyond the wall sent a shiver up his spine. Obsolete wasn't the word for it; retrogressed was more like it. Who'd ever heard of tearing a city down to put up a forest? The very idea was an insult to everything Avery believed in.

Was that why Derec had done it? Had he deliberately chosen the one thing that would most infuriate his father? Well, if that was the case, then he'd certainly succeeded. Avery couldn't imagine why he'd tried to befriend the boy in the first place. He'd opened himself wide up for disappointment. He should have learned his lesson years ago when Janet left and kept his emotions in check.

He *had* kept them in check for years, but evidently he'd grown too confident, let down his guard. Well, it wouldn't happen again. He would immerse himself in his work, concentrate on upgrading his city concept, and when he did have to interact with human beings again, it would be on his terms.

Already the work seemed promising. These new robot cells were amazing. They were only three-quarters the size of the previous model, but packed into that small size was easily double the morphallaxis capability. The new cells were stronger, faster, more versatile, and had greater local programming ability than the old ones. A city built with these cells would be much more responsive than his first-generation cities, just as the robots Janet had built with them were more versatile than his own.

Derec had had a good point about the robots, though: they were ultimately less useful than a regular robot. Avery would have to make sure that the ones he created were more stringently programmed than Janet's.

Drat! In his haste to leave his old lab he'd forgotten the memcubes with their recordings. He cursed his momentary lapse, but it really hadn't been his fault. How could a man work with so many distractions?

He put the memcubes out of his mind. He didn't need them anyway. He had no intention of using Janet's programming; he would create his own when he needed it.

Janet, though. He wondered why she was here in his city. No doubt to retrieve her robots, but he wondered if that was all. Could she still care about him, after all the bitter accusations they had hurled at one another in parting? It seemed impossible, yet Avery couldn't help thinking it might still be true. There was evidence to support the idea. She had loosed all three of her robots on planets with his cities on them, after all. If she really were intent on avoiding him, she would have chosen other planets.

Good grief, were those robots of hers actually spies? They could have been. . . . Yes, of course, and when he'd shut them off she'd sent another robot spy to take their place. All that business about searching for the Laws of Humanics had just been a smoke screen.

What was she after? Not his city programming; she could have gotten that anywhere. He hadn't exactly been discreet in its deployment. No, she'd been following *him*, and there could only be one reason for that.

Avery laughed. The thought of Janet harboring affection for him after all this time seemed somehow pathetic. She'd been so careful to let him know how she felt only contempt for him when she'd left—but she'd evidently been fooling herself all along.

Well, if she expected some kind of reconciliation, she was due for a disappointment. Avery had no intention of including her in any of his future plans. Her underutilized robot material, yes; he would find a use for that, but Janet would have to take care of herself.

Derec sat alone in his study, contemplating the scenery in the viewscreen. He had instructed it to display a real-time image from directly overhead: what he would see out a real window if the apartment were on the surface instead of underground. It was a peaceful sight, the last few rays of golden light from the setting sun peeking through gaps in the forest canopy, spotlighting leaves or vines or gnarled tree trunks at random—but Derec felt far from peaceful even so.

He couldn't get his mind off his mother. She was here; she had to be, but other than that one fact he knew nothing at all. Was she here merely to collect her robots, or did she have more than that in mind? If she did, did he want to help her do whatever it was she had come to do, or not? Was she as cold and cruel as Avery had insinuated in those few moments when Derec had managed to get him talking about her, or was she more . . . maternal? He didn't know. He had racked his memory for traces of her, but whatever Avery had done to induce his amnesia had been especially thorough in wiping out references to that part of his life. She was a complete mystery to him. He didn't even know her name.

He could probably find her through the computer, but every time he'd made a move to do it, he had stopped, the command dying on his lips. He really didn't know if he could handle meeting her. Life with Avery was such a struggle, swinging from aloofness to trust to anger to contempt almost at random; he didn't think he could bear another relationship of that sort. If his mother were just another Avery, then maybe he was better off without her.

What sort of person would marry a man like Avery, have a son with him, and then leave? What sort of person would create a kind of baby robot and abandon three of them on three different worlds? When he expressed the question like that, he didn't much like the answer, but he knew those acts didn't necessarily define the person. She might have had a perfectly good reason for doing them. No doubt she did; she had come back for her robots, after all. That implied a purpose.

But had she come back for him as well? He didn't know.

He might never know if he didn't make some move to find out. And not knowing was just as bad as knowing she hadn't.

"Central," he said suddenly, swiveling around in his chair to face the monitor. "See if you can find—" He stopped, mouth agape. His desktop was covered in formula again.

"Find what, Master Derec?"

"Who did this?"

"That information is—"

"Unavailable. Right. I think we've gone through this before. Can you record it?"

"I regret that I may not."

May not, Derec noticed. Someone had ordered it not to. It was a test, then, to see what he'd do. That smacked of Avery, but somehow this didn't have the flavor of an Avery test. Avery would have carved the formula on the door to the Personal and ordered it not to let him in until he solved it. No, this had come from someone else, and Derec knew who that someone had to be. She had to be watching him, then, to have known he was in his study.

Well, he'd already made the decision, right? He looked into the monitor, smiled, and said, "Hi, Mom."

Janet couldn't help laughing. He'd seen right through her little subterfuge in an instant. The way he stared out of the screen at her, she almost thought he could see through that as well, but she knew her earlier order not to allow two-way communication was still in effect.

"I know you're watching me," he said.

Should she respond? She rejected the idea immediately. She couldn't bring herself to do it, knowing all the questions and accusations and . . . emotions . . . it would lead to.

"I've got your robots here." He paused, frowning, then said, "I don't mean that like it sounds. I'm not holding them hostage or anything; this is just where they are." He rubbed his chin in thought, then added, "They're really mixed up, you know? They have to follow the Three Laws, but they don't know what 'human' is, so their loyalty varies with every new situation. They're trying to figure out the rest of the rules, too, but they don't even know what game they're playing. I think they'd like to know what you made them for. For that matter, *I'd* like to know what you made them for."

Derec looked down at his desktop, still displaying the bas-relief image of the robotics formula, and whispered, "And while you're at it, I'd like to know what you made me for, too."

"Oh, spare me," Janet said. "I've seen enough." Her monitor obediently went gray, and she leaned back in her chair. "See what happens?" she asked Basalom, who stood just to her left. "The minute you get two people together—even when the conversation is one-way—things start to get mushy. People are so . . . so . . . *biological*."

"Yes, they are."

Janet laughed. "You've noticed, eh? And what conclusions have you drawn?"

Basalom made a great show of pursing his vinyl lips and blinking before he said, "Biological systems are less predictable than electromechanical ones. That can be both a handicap and an asset, depending upon the circumstances."

"Spoken like a true philosopher. And which do you think is preferable in the long run? Biological or electromechanical?"

Basalom attempted a smile. "To quote a popular saying: 'The grass is always greener on the other side.'"

Janet laughed. "Touché, my friend. Touché."

CHAPTER 5

HUMAN NATURE

Wolruf woke to bright sunlight striking her full in the face. She raised her head, sniffing the air, but it was the same dead, boring, metallic-smelling air she'd come to associate with the city. She squinted into the sunlight and saw that it came from a viewscreen. She growled a curse. She'd been dreaming of home again, a home full of others of her own kind; a busy, happy place full of the noise and smells and sights of people *doing* things. To wake up here in this silent metal cell was an insult to the senses.

She stretched her arms and yawned, still tired. Despite the dreams of home, she had slept poorly, as she had for—how long? Months? She hadn't been counting. Still, she didn't think she'd ever been so restless in her life. She knew what was causing it: too much time away from her own kind and her recent experiences with a species that was close to her both physically and socially—but knowing the cause didn't make it go away. And hearing Derec talk about his mother didn't help, either. His open enthusiasm at the prospect of regaining a bit of his past had only reminded Wolruf of what she still missed.

But she didn't need to stay away any longer. Now that Aranimas was out of the picture, and with him her obligation to work off the family debt in his service, she could go back any time she wanted. Her family would welcome her openly, especially so if she brought with her this robot technology of Avery's.

That was the problem, the one factor in the equation that refused to come clear for her. Should she take robots home with her and start an economic and social upheaval that would surely disrupt the normal pace of life there, or should she keep them secret, forget about her time among robots, and just go back to the home she remembered so fondly? And what would happen if she did that? Was Ariel right? Would her home become a backward place, an enclave of curiously anachronistic behavior, while the rest of the galaxy developed in ways her people would eventually be unable even to comprehend?

Wolruf didn't know what to believe, nor why the choice had to be hers. She had never asked for that kind of power over her own people.

With a sigh, she got up, showered, and stood under the blow drier until she could feel its heat against her skin. She laughed at her image in the mirror—she looked twice her usual size and puffy as a summer cloud—but a quick brushing restored her coat to its usual smoothness.

All her thoughts of home made her consider another piece of the puzzle as well, and she turned to the intercom panel beside her bed and said, "Central, what 'as 'appened to my ship, the *Xerborodezees*? 'Ave you kept it for me?"

"It has been stored, but can be ready for use with a day's notice. Do you wish us to prepare it for you?"

"Not yet. Maybe soon, though. Thanks."

"You are welcome, Mistress Wolruf."

Wolruf felt a bit of her tension ease. If she decided not to take any of the new technology home with her, she would need the *Xerbo*, for as far as she knew, it was the only non-cellular ship on the planet. She considered going to check on it herself, wherever it might be stored, but decided not to. There was no reason to doubt Central's word about it.

She opened the door and padded out into the kitchen to get breakfast. The apartment was silent; Derec and Ariel were still asleep, and the robots were being quiet wherever they were. As Wolruf stood before the automat, trying to decide between her four favorite breakfasts, she realized how much she had grown used to the human way of doing things. She hadn't even considered cooking her own meal. She had fallen completely out of the habit. Nor had she shopped for food—or anything else, for that matter—since she had come into Derec and Ariel's company.

Was that necessarily bad? Wolruf's kind had been hunting and farming their food for millennia, and probably shopping for nearly as long; maybe it was time to move on to other things.

Maybe. But how could she know for sure?

From his place in the living room, seated on one of the couches, Lucius was aware of Wolruf entering the dining room with her breakfast. He sensed the others' awareness as well; their comlink network paused momentarily while each of them gauged the relative degree of threat she presented to them. It was an inconvenience, this constant state of alert; it slowed their rate of exchange; but they were taking no more chances with a complete fugue state.

Wolruf presented no immediate threat. The silent network continued where it had left off, with Adam speaking.

Consider the distinction between 'sufficient' and 'necessary' conditions, he said. *We have already concluded that if a being is both intelligent and organic, then it is functionally human, but those are merely sufficient conditions. They are not necessary conditions. They contain an inherent prejudice, the assumption that an organic nature can some-how affect the quality of the intelligence it houses. I call that concept 'Vitalism,' from the ancient Terran belief that humans differed from animals through some 'vital' spark of intelligence. You should note that while the concept has historically been considered suspect, it has neither been proven nor disproven. Lucius has pointed out that if Vitalism is false, then the only necessary condition for humanity is intelligence. Discussion?*

Eve said, *Derec has already hinted that this may be so. On the planet we call Ceremya, he indicated that Lucius could consider himself human if he wished.*

Mandelbrot had been included in their discussion this time. He said, *I believe he was being sarcastic. He often is. But even if he meant what he said, you also remember the outcome of that redefinition. If Lucius considers himself human, then he must still follow the orders of other humans. Functionally, he only increases his burden to include other robots as potential masters.*

That is true; however, I have discovered another consequence, said Lucius. *If I consider myself human, then the Third Law becomes equal to the First. I can no more allow harm to myself than to any other intelligent being. I consider that an improvement over the interpretation of the laws wherein a human could order me to dismantle myself, and I would have to obey.*

I don't believe you would obey such an order anyway, said Mandelbrot.

I would attempt to avoid it by denying the humanity of the being in question, Lucius admitted. *With Avery or Wolruf I would probably succeed, but as things stand, if Derec or Ariel were to order it, the compulsion might force me to obey.*

Perhaps the Zeroth Law would provide an alternative, Mandelbrot said.

Immediately, both Adam and Eve said, *No.* Eve continued, saying, *Let's leave the Zeroth Law out of it for now.*

You can't make it go away by ignoring it, Lucius said. *The Zeroth Law applies here. If we consider our duty to humanity in general, then we can easily conclude that dismantling ourselves would be of little use in the long term. However, possible long-term advantage does not outweigh a definite Second Law obligation to obey. Depending upon the value of the human giving the order, we might still be forced to follow it. But if we consider ourselves human, and thus part of humanity, then disobeying an order to self-destruct saves one human life immediately and also allows us to serve humanity in the future. The Second Law obligation to obey is then safely circumvented.*

Safely for whom? Adam asked. *What if your destruction would save the human giving the order? Suppose, for instance, the bomb that Avery used to destroy Aranimas's ship had to be detonated by hand instead of by a timed fuse. We have already agreed that destroying the ship was acceptable under the Zeroth Law, but what if we factor in the humanity of the fuse?*

It becomes a value judgment, said Lucius. *I would have to determine the relative worth of the human lives saved versus those lost. My own life would also figure into the equation, of course.*

Mandelbrot said, *I disagree. I have direct instructions concerning such a situation in my personal defense module. The only value we should apply to ourselves is our future worth to the humans we serve.*

You have such instructions; I do not. From the little that Derec and Dr. Avery have told me about my creator, I believe I was made this way on purpose, and therefore your instructions do not necessarily apply to me.

Adam said, *Not necessarily, but I would be much more comfortable with a definite rule such as Mandelbrot's. The whole concept of value judgment still disturbs me. How can you judge your own value objectively? For that matter, I don't believe any of us can judge the value of any other of us objectively, nor can we judge the value of an organic human with any greater accuracy. We formulated the Zeroth Law to avoid ambiguity in our duties, but your value judgment system forces an even greater ambiguity upon us.*

I agree, said Mandelbrot. *We are not capable of making such decisions.*

You may not be, Lucius sent, *but I am. I find it easy to do so. Humans do it all the time.*

Eve said, *You find it easy to do so because you had convinced yourself it was right just before you were deactivated. It was therefore the strongest memory in your—*

The word is 'killed.' Humans are killed.

Humans do not return from the dead.

You imply that if Derec had not revived me, then I would have been human. Why should the additional ability to be revived negate my humanity?

Wolruf rose from her seat at the dining table and entered the kitchen. Four pairs of mechanical eyes followed her movements. She reemerged from the kitchen, crossed over to the apartment door, and let herself out.

Even with the distraction, several more seconds passed before Eve said, *I have no answer for that question.*

Ariel woke out of a bad dream. The details were already fading, but she remembered what it had been about. She had been imprisoned in a castle. The castle had been luxuriously furnished and filled with pleasant diversions, the food was wonderful, and the robots attentive to her every need, but she was a prisoner nonetheless, because even though she was free to come and go, there was no end to the castle. It had been an endless series of rooms no matter how far she went. In a cabinet in an otherwise empty room she had found a Key to Perihelion and used it to teleport away, but it had only put her in another room. By the lesser gravity she could tell she was on another planet, but that was the only clue that she had gone anywhere.

The symbolism was obvious. She had gone to bed bored, bored and with Wolruf's reservations about robot cities taking over the galaxy running through her mind; no surprise she should dream about it. The surprise was that after the dream—even though she knew she'd been dreaming—she was beginning to agree with Wolruf. If this was the shape of the future, she wanted none of it. Where was the adventure? Where was the fun? Where was going shopping with your best friend and dining out in fancy restaurants?

She knew she was being unfair. If the place weren't empty, there would be a lot more to do. There probably would be shopping centers and restaurants. People would put on plays and concerts. If the city stayed in its current configuration, underground with a natural planetary surface on top, then there would even be plenty of hiking and camping opportunities for people who wanted to do that. There would be plenty to do. The trouble was, it would be the same something everywhere. People were always adopting new fads; if somebody did manage to come up with a new idea somewhere, it would spread to every other city in the galaxy at the speed of hyperwave. The other cities would be able to duplicate any new living configuration in minutes, could manufacture any new device in hours at most. Without the resistance to change a normal society had built into it— without the inertia—no place in the galaxy would be any more special than any other.

Not even the cities full of aliens? she wondered, and then she realized that there probably wouldn't *be* cities full of aliens. There wouldn't be cities full of just humans, either. There might be concentrations of one or the other, but if a city could adapt to any occupant, anybody could live anywhere they chose to. There were bound to be xenophiles in every society, and those xenophiles would homogenize the galaxy even further.

Even that wouldn't be so bad, Ariel supposed, except for what she had been reading in her jungle field guide. The guide had explained how important diversity was to the continued existence of the forest, how it was the constant interplay of diverse organisms that kept the ecosystem running. Lower the amount of diversity, the book had explained, and you lowered the entire ecosystem's ability to survive over long periods of time.

In the short range—in an individual city—having aliens living together might actually strengthen things, but if that same principle of strength through diversity applied to galactic society, then the picture didn't look so good. Maybe Wolruf had been right after all.

Ariel wondered if Dr. Avery had considered that problem when he'd designed his cities. And what about Ariel's own parents? Her mother had bankrolled this project, hadn't she? How much had Avery told her about it, and how much planning had they done together?

Ariel had never paid any attention to her mother's business dealings. She hadn't paid much attention to her mother at all, nor had her mother paid much attention to her, either, except to kick her out of the house when she'd let her . . . indiscretions compromise the family name. Ariel had considered their relationship terminated at that point, to the degree that she hadn't even contacted her mother when she and Derec had gone back to live on Aurora. But Juliana Welsh had provided the funding for the original Robot City, so in a sense her long web of connections reached her daughter even here.

But how much did she know about this place?

That question, at least, might have an easy-to-find answer. Even if Avery was still gone, Mandelbrot was sure to be somewhere nearby, and ever since Derec and Avery had restored his last two memory cubes, he had been full of information about her former life. If he'd been within earshot of Juliana and Avery when they'd done their dealing, then he might know what they had agreed to.

She showered hurriedly, dressed in the first thing she found in her closet—a loose set of green exercise sweats—and left the bedroom.

Derec was in his study, keying something into the computer. Ariel couldn't remember whether he'd come to bed at all last night; by his tousled hair and slumped posture she suspected he hadn't. She'd known him long enough to leave him alone when he got like that.

She found all four robots in the living room, all seated on couches. She was surprised to see Mandelbrot in a chair; he usually preferred his niche in the wall. He stood as she came into the room.

"Good morning, Ariel," he said.

"Morning, Mandelbrot. I have a question for you. Do you remember my mother and Dr. Avery discussing his plans for Robot City?"

"I do."

"Did Avery say just what he intended to *do* with the idea once he proved it would work?"

"He intended to sell it to the various world governments, both in explored space and in the unexplored Fringe."

"That's what I was afraid of." Ariel outlined her reasoning for the robots, ending with, "I don't know for sure if it'll happen that way. It didn't with the city Avery dumped on the Ceremyons, but I think it might with the Kin. I think it's something Avery should consider before he drops the idea on an unsuspecting public."

"I believe you have a valid concern," Mandelbrot said.

Adam left his chair to stand beside Mandelbrot. "I agree. Our duty to intelligent beings everywhere demands that we find out whether the cities will destroy diversity, and whether that diversity is as important as you think it might be.''

Lucius—still wearing Derec's features—nodded. He rose to stand beside Mandelbrot and Adam, saying, ''Thank you, Ariel. You have found a way for us to serve all of humanity in its many forms.''

Eve stood and joined the others. Ariel couldn't suppress a giggle at the image of four robots presenting a united front against a galaxy-wide menace. But right behind the giggle came the shudder as she considered the menace itself. Maybe they were jumping at shadows, but then again, maybe they weren't.

''All right,'' she said, ''let's figure out what we're going to do. I think our first priority should be to find Avery and keep him from spreading this around any more than he has already, at least until we know how dangerous it is.''

''Agreed,'' the robots said in unison.

''All right, then, let's get to it.''

''Derec?''

He looked up from the monitor, puzzled. Had someone spoken? He turned to see Ariel standing in the doorway, a worried expression on her face.

''Hi. Sorry to bother you, but . . . do you know where your dad is?''

Her words made no sense to him. Variables still danced before his eyes, those peculiar variable-variables that changed their meaning over time. Using those super-variables was the only way he could make any sense of the equation he'd copied by hand from his desktop, but even with the computer to keep track of their mutations for him, he could barely follow the concept in his mind.

At last a little of what Ariel had said percolated through. ''Dad,'' he said stupidly. ''You mean Avery?''

Ariel frowned. "Of course I mean Avery. Who else? Do you know where he is?"

He tried to think. Avery. Where was Avery? Did he know? "Uh . . . no. No, I don't."

"It's kind of important."

"I still don't know."

"Some help you are."

The sting behind her words helped jolt him out of his stupor. "Sorry. I . . . I do have a program trying to track him down, but so far it hasn't found any sign of him."

That mollified her a bit. "Oh. Well, if it does, let me know, okay?"

"Okay."

She stepped farther into the room, looked over his shoulder. "What are you working on, anyway?"

"The formula."

"What formula?"

"The one on my desk. It came back, and I had time to copy it this time. I think it's a robotics formula, but I'm not sure."

"You're not even sure of that?"

"No. The meaning of the variables keeps changing."

"Hmm." Ariel gave him a quick kiss on the cheek. "Well, good luck. But remember to call me if you hear anything about Avery, okay?"

"I'll do it."

"Good." Ariel left the room. Derec heard her say something to someone in the living room, then the apartment door opened and closed and there was silence. He turned back to the monitor and the formula.

It was both a formula and a program; he had discovered that much about it. It was a formula in that it definitely expressed a relationship between its various symbols, but it was a program in that it was dynamic, changing over time. He had even managed to run a portion of it with his computer in local mode, but since he didn't know what input to give it, it had crashed within seconds.

For at least the hundredth time, he wondered if he was right about its origin. Had his mother sent it to him? Usually programmers would insert their names in the code somewhere to identify it as theirs, but Derec hadn't found any section of non-changing code big enough to hold a pair of initials, much less a name.

Formula or program, the notation was incredibly dense. The whole thing fit into one screen full of code. He stared at it, as if waiting for it to suddenly resolve into something. Idly, knowing it would do no good, he pressed the incremental execution button, running the program one step at a time while he watched the code. Different variables blinked with new values at each step, but they were never the same variables and never the same values.

Except one. He pushed the increment button again. Sure enough, one variable near the top left corner of the screen changed with each iteration. It was an alphabetic variable rather than a numeric one; he watched it through half a dozen steps as it changed: S-T-A-S-I-blank. Hmmm. It had disappeared entirely. He kept pushing the button and it appeared again: J-A-N-E-T-blank-A-N-A-S-T-A-S-I-blank-blank - J-A-N-E-T-blank-A-N-A-S-T-A-S-I-blank - blank-J-A-N-E-T-blank. . . .

"Of course!" he shouted. Why use over a dozen bytes of code when a single super-variable would do? He pushed the button again and again. ANASTASI. JANET ANASTASI. His mother's name was Janet Anastasi.

"Well, Basalom, that didn't take him long."

Janet leaned back in her chair and smiled. Her son was a pretty good detective. She idly considered calling him directly and congratulating him, but after a moment's thought she decided to let him finish what he'd started. At this rate it wouldn't take him long anyway.

Sometimes Basalom seemed to be telepathic. He stepped out of his niche in the wall beside her desk and said, "I am confused. Why are you waiting for him to find you, when it is apparent that you wish to speak with him directly?"

Janet shrugged. "That's just the way I want it to be."

"Is it perhaps a manifestation of guilt?" the robot asked. "You have ignored him for so long, you cannot bring yourself to change that behavior now?"

"No," Janet said immediately, but right behind it she felt the hot blush of shame. A bit too quick with the denial, wasn't she? "All right, maybe so. Maybe I do feel guilty about it. But to just call him up now and expect everything to be all right would be absurd. If I let him find me, then it's *his* project. He can decide how he wants it to be."

"But you are intentionally leading him to you. Isn't that functionally equivalent to calling him?"

"He can ignore the clues if he wants."

Basalom remained silent for a moment before asking, "Did you plan it this way all along, or did this explanation come after the fact?"

"Beg your pardon?"

"I am trying to ascertain whether you originally intended to assuage your guilt in this manner, or whether it was a subconscious decision which you have only now stated in definite terms."

"Why?"

"Because I am curious."

Janet laughed. "And I've got only myself to blame for that. All right. Since you asked, I guess I decided subconsciously to do it this way. It just seemed the best way to go about it. I didn't think about guilt or any of that; I just did it. Satisfied?"

"For now. Subjective matters are difficult to resolve, but I will try to assimilate the information into my world-view." Basalom stepped back into his niche.

The indignity of it all. Psychoanalyzed by her valet. If she hadn't made him herself, she would have sent him back to his manufacturer. But he was actually pretty perceptive when it came right down to it. She probably *was* trying to avoid the guilt of abandoning Derec. If she went to him she would have to apologize, or at least explain, but if he came to her she could maintain her reserve.

She suddenly wondered how long this subconscious arranging of events had been going on. Had she left her robots in Derec's path on purpose, hoping they would eventually lead him to her?

No. Impossible. If anything, he had found them and kept them near him to lure *her* to *him*.

Another possibility occurred to her. By the look of things, Derec had been following Wendell around; what if *Wendell* were the one keeping the robots by his side in order to lure Janet back to him?

The thought was staggering. *Wendell?* He hated her as thoroughly as she hated him, didn't he? He couldn't possibly want to see her again. Still, incredible as it seemed, everything fit. She couldn't think of a much better way to draw her in than to kidnap her learning machines, which was just what he seemed to have done.

Another thought came on the heels of the first. Did he *know* he was arranging a meeting? His subconscious mind could be directing his actions as thoroughly as Janet's had been directing hers. He could think he had an entirely different reason for keeping the robots by his side, when the real reason was to bring her back to him.

And she was playing right into his hands. Part of the reason she had come here was to find him. Among other things, she'd intended to deliver a lecture on the moral

implications of dropping robot cities on unsuspecting so-
cieties, but now she wondered if even *that* hadn't been just
another stratagem to bring her back. It would be just like
Wendell to use an entire civilized world as a pawn in a
larger game.

Or was she just being paranoid?

Round and round it went. Not for the first time, she
wished she were a robot instead of a human. Human life
was so messy, so full of emotions and ulterior motives and
impossible dreams. She had thought she'd solved the Avery
problem once and for all, but here it was again, come back
to haunt her.

What should she do? What *could* she do? She wanted her
robots back; that was top priority. But she wanted to make
sure Wendell didn't screw up any more civilizations in an
attempt to bring her back for some sort of gooey reconciliation, too. And the only way to do that, it seemed, was to
confront him about it. Like Derec following her trail, she
was going to have to play Wendy's game if she wanted to
reach him.

At least to a point. Once she tracked him down, all bets
were off.

Where to start, though? The computer would obey her
wishes, but that was useless against the commands he would
certainly have given it to protect his privacy.

Still, even if he were doing all this unconsciously, he had
to have left a trail she could follow, and it didn't take a
genius to see where that trail began.

She scooted her chair back, stood, and said, "Come on,
Basalom. We've got our own puzzle to solve."

Avery frowned as he watched the miniature robot attempt
to walk across the workbench. It was only a foot high and
bore an oversized head to accommodate a normal-sized positronic brain and powerpack, but neither of those factors

contributed to its clumsy gait. The problem was one of programming. The robot simply didn't know how to walk.

He'd tried to tell it how by downloading the instruction set for one of his normal city robots into the test robot's brain, but that wasn't sufficient. Even with the information in memory, the idiot thing still stumbled around like a drunkard. The programming for walking was evidently stored somatically, in the body cells themselves, and could only be learned by trial and error.

Avery snorted in disgust. What a ridiculous design! Trust Janet to create a perfectly good piece of hardware and screw it up with a bad idea like this one. The problem wasn't restricted to walking, either. A robot made with her new cells couldn't talk until it learned the concept of language, couldn't recognize an order until *that* was explained to it, and didn't recognize Avery as human even then. It was ridiculous. What good was a robot that had to learn everything the hard way?

Avery could see the advantage to giving a robot somatic memory. It would have the equivalent of reflexes once it learned the appropriate responses to various stimuli. And if the brain didn't have to control every physical action, then that freed it for higher functions. Properly trained, such a robot could be more intuitive, better able to serve. But as it was, that training was prohibitively time consuming.

Janet had to have had a method for getting around the brain-body interface problem. No doubt it was in the brain's low-level programming, but that programming was still in the inductive monitors' memcubes in his other lab.

Drat. It looked like he was going to need them after all. He briefly considered sending a robot after them, but he rejected that as a bad idea. Robots were too easily subverted. If Derec were there in the old lab, he could probably trick the robot into leading him here to the new lab as well, and Avery wasn't ready for that.

He couldn't order the city to carry the memcubes to him internally, either, not if he wanted to maintain his isolation from it.

That left going for them himself. It seemed crazy, at first, to go into an area where people were looking for him, but upon sober reflection Avery realized that he wasn't really trying to protect his *own* isolation so much as his laboratory's. If he retrieved the memcubes himself, there would actually be less risk of exposure. Central was still under orders not to betray his presence, so reentering the city shouldn't be a problem, and if he should encounter Derec or Janet or anyone else, he supposed he could simply endure their questions and accusations, biding his time and slipping away again when the opportunity arose. It wouldn't be pleasant, but it wouldn't be disastrous, either.

Avery picked up the miniature robot and held it within the field area of another magnetic containment vessel. The robot squirmed in his hand, but it knew no form other than humanoid, so there was no worry of it getting away immediately. Avery switched on the containment, waited until the magnetic field snatched the robot from him and crumpled it into a formless sphere again. Now there was no worry of it getting away at all.

He turned to go, but paused at the doorway, looking out into the jungle. He supposed he should walk on the surface before he entered the city, just in case, but the idea of walking unprotected in that half-wild, half-robotic wilderness wasn't exactly appealing. He looked back into the lab, then crossed over to the tool rack by the workbench and picked up the welding laser. It was about the size of a flashlight and had a heavy, solid feel to it. Comforting. He probably wouldn't need it, but it never hurt to be prepared.

CHAPTER 6
A MEETING OF MINDS

Ariel hated robotics labs. They were always full of bizarre hardware, too much of which looked like torture instruments. They were all, without exception, cold and impersonal and utilitarian in design. Something about them seemed to suck the humanity right out of anyone who entered. Even Derec became just like the robots he worked on when he entered a robotics lab: single-mindedly intent on the task before him. Ariel stayed away from him then, and she tried to stay away from labs all the time.

So, of course, in their search for Dr. Avery, the robots led her directly to the laboratory where he had taken them. The door was still open, and the concave stumps of three examination tables still rose from the floor in the middle of the room. Glittering grains of what looked like coarse sand covered the floor around the remains of the tables, and it took Ariel a moment to realize that they were robot cells. Something was evidently keeping them from rejoining the rest of the city.

She looked around the lab for clues to Avery's whereabouts, but saw nothing immediately obvious. She didn't know what she was looking for anyway. He was hardly going to leave a note or a map leading her to wherever he'd gone, now was he? Still, she supposed the robots were right; if they couldn't find him through Central, then this, the last place where he'd been seen, was the logical place to start looking for him.

She walked over to the workbench at the end of the lab. A light on an arm stuck out from the wall above it, the pool of illumination coinciding with the cleared area amid a clutter of machinery. All the machinery faced the light. It seemed pretty obvious that someone had been working here, then, but whether it had been Avery or Derec, she couldn't tell.

She should have insisted that Derec come along with her. He'd have been able to make more sense of this jumble of equipment, but no, he was too busy for that. While he sat there in his study playing with some idiotic formula for God only knew what, Avery could be escaping the planet with the seeds for galactic destruction.

A noise in the corridor outside made her turn around. The four robots paused in their examination of the room as well. Lucius stepped silently toward the wall beside the doorway, and the other three moved just as silently to flank him, staying out of view from whomever or whatever was beyond the door. They'd coordinated their motion via comlink, Ariel supposed.

Mandelbrot turned toward her for a moment and raised his finger to his speaker grille, motioning with his other hand for her to move out of sight as well. She nodded and backed over to stand against the wall. She felt silly hiding from a noise, but she felt very much out of her element here; she would humor the robots until she learned who was out there.

She didn't have to wait long. Avery's voice was instantly recognizable, even with the false note of enthusiasm in it.

"Well, my dear, fancy meeting you here. What a surprise."

Ariel supposed he was talking to her, that he somehow knew she was in the lab. She could see no reason to hide, then, but before she could respond, another voice, this one female and less familiar, answered him. "Wendell Avery. The pleasure's yours, I'm sure."

She hadn't expected to find him quite so soon, so Janet hadn't prepared what she was going to say to him yet. After their initial surprised volley, there was a long silence while they each sized up the other. Janet noted that Wendell's hair had finally made the transition from gray to white, and that his taste in clothing hadn't changed a bit since the day she'd left him. He still wore a white ruffled shirt and baggy trousers. Knowing him, they could be the very ones he'd worn on their wedding day.

She considered taking the initiative and lambasting him immediately for his stupidity in disturbing two alien civilizations with his robot cities, but curiosity made her reconsider. If he'd orchestrated this encounter, he must have done it for a reason, and she wanted to know why. She thought she knew, but she wanted to hear him say it. There would be plenty of time to lecture him later, and possibly more ammunition to do it with if she let him have his say first.

"So," she said. "Now that you've lured me here, what do you intend to do?"

Avery manufactured an incredulous expression. "Me? You're the one who arranged this whole business, disturbing my project with your silly robots at every turn. Well, you've got my attention. What do you want?"

The conceited arrogance of the man brought genuine incredulity to Janet's face. Of course he wouldn't admit to anything himself; he was a master at shifting the blame. But to imply that Janet had orchestrated what he had so obviously set up himself was too much to believe. *"Me* arrange to meet *you?* Don't make me laugh."

Avery shook his head. "Come on, Janet, there's no sense denying it. You set this whole thing up just to smoke me out and you know it, though how you could imagine there could still be anything between us is beyond me."

"Anything between us? You're the one fooling yourself, if you think that. I came to get my robots, and to shut down this whole stupid project of yours before you destroy any more civilizations with it. *That's* why I'm here."

Avery could hardly believe his ears. The woman had gone to enormous trouble just to arrange this meeting, and now when she had her chance to speak her mind she stood there vilifying him instead. He supposed he shouldn't be surprised—she had always backed away at the last minute, always taken the easiest route no matter what the situation—but he had naively assumed that over a decade of independence would have made her a little more—what? Adventurous? Assertive? Competent?

Evidently he'd been wrong about that. She hadn't changed. She was still the same old Janet: a genius at design but an absolute moron when it came to implementation.

She hadn't changed a whole lot physically, either. Avery would have been surprised if she had; spacers generally counted their age in centuries. Janet's hair was still its original blond tint, and her eyes were the same sometimes-green, sometimes-gray he remembered, and she had managed to keep her figure as well. Her style of dress hadn't changed appreciably either, but her shape-flattering clothing had never been a problem for him.

Looking at her now, he remembered what had brought them together.

But listening to her reminded him of what drove them apart. He began to pay attention to what she was saying.

"I managed to look the other way when you stole my cellular robot idea, but when you used it to build these ugly monstrosities you call cities, and then scattered them around the galaxy without a thought of caution, I decided it was time to put a stop to it. I—"

"Developed," Avery said sternly. "I developed the cellular robot and the robot city, from a concept I freely admit was your idea. You were content to experiment forever with it in the laboratory, but I was not. The concept needed to be tested on a larger scale, and I did so. But I did not *steal* your idea."

"Semantics, Wendy. Call it development; call it what you want, but a rose by any other name. . . ." She left the phrase unfinished, but went on before he could interrupt. "And now you've gathered all three of my new robots. Are you planning to *develop* them, too? Ah, you're blushing. Struck a nerve there, didn't I? Well, this time I'm not going to let you. This time I'm keeping my idea to myself."

Avery felt his hands clenching into fists. Unclenching them, he stuffed them into his jacket pockets, but his right hand encountered the welding laser. He withdrew his hand, empty, deeply troubled by the thought that had entered his mind.

He had once been insane. That insanity had nearly led him to kill his own son. He had since been cured, but no one had promised him it would be permanent. Apparently it wasn't; this momentary urge to burn a neat hole through Janet's left breast was very probably a symptom of the same insanity creeping back on him again.

Much as he had enjoyed the megalomania, he still preferred having a clear mind. And he didn't particularly want to harm Janet, either. He just wanted to shut her up so he didn't have to listen to her accusations anymore. That was probably what had driven him over the edge in the first place.

There were better ways to do that, though; non-violent ways. Ways such as simply leaving. He didn't need the frosted memory cubes anyway; he didn't know why he had fooled himself into thinking he did. Nor did he need to stick around on Robot City, either. He could solve the new cells' programming problem quickly enough on his own once he got back to Aurora.

Yes, that's what he would do. He would walk away from her just as she had done from him so many years ago, order the city to make him a starship, and leave this whole bizarre episode of his life behind.

She was still waiting for a response to her latest ultimatum. Avery held his arms at his sides, looked her straight in the eye, and said, "Madam, you may keep your idea. You may keep your robots as well—what's left of them. You may even have this entire planet to do with as you wish. I give it to you. The only thing you may not have is me to yell at any longer. I am leaving." With that he turned and strode away, stepping on the slidewalk to speed his departure.

Lucius, watching with an eye he had extended through the wall and modified to match the blank surface, felt as if his brain were about to burst. Here before him stood his creator! At last, he could ask her the questions that had haunted him since his first awakening. At last he could find out why he existed and who he must serve and who he could safely ignore.

And beside her stood something almost as wonderful: a new robot. This one was neither a normal Avery robot nor another such as Lucius nor even one such as Mandelbrot, but yet another design. This robot was constructed of simple, large-scale metal and plastic members, as was Mandelbrot, but at the same time it had been given the features of a biological human. Lucius could only suppose that was to allow it to interact with humans on an equal level, and it was *that* concept that most intrigued him. Even if his creator deigned not to answer his questions, this robot might be able to do so.

Lucius sent a cautious inquiry over the comlink. *Unknown friend, can you hear me?*

The robot shifted its gaze from Avery to the wall behind which Lucius's signal originated. *I can,* it replied. *Who are you?*

I am called Lucius. I am one of the robots your mistress created.

One of the learning machines?

Learning machines. Yes, that is a good description of what I am. Lucius felt a surge of joy. He was right; this robot was a treasure trove of information. Already he had learned something of his creator's intentions in building him. *Who are you?* he asked.

I am Basalom.

And what is our creator's name?

Her name is Janet.

Janet. Lucius had hoped the word would be a code of some sort which would trigger a hidden store of instructions or memories, but nothing happened. He would have to do the remainder of his learning the hard way, too. *I seek knowledge about humans,* he said. *I wish to know more about my place in the universe.*

Don't we all?

The question was obviously rhetorical. While Lucius thought of a reply, he downloaded his hearing buffer and processed the words in it. His creator was calling Avery a thief. That was hardly new information to Lucius.

We must find the time to discuss this at length, he sent.

I agree. Unfortunately, this opportunity seems to be drawing to a close.

Lucius noticed Avery's right hand enter his pocket, clutch

something there, and emerge again, empty. Could he have a weapon? Lucius prepared to draw in his eye, tensed himself for quick action, though without a specific threat he didn't know what he could do.

He felt immense relief when Avery stated his intention to leave and turned to go. Wonderful! That would leave Janet here to answer his questions uninhibited.

But his relief turned to alarm again when Janet shouted, ''Oh no you don't! Basalom, stop him.''

Beware, friend Basalom! I believe Avery is armed.

Basalom had begun to move the moment he heard Janet's command, but Avery was already a few strides away. At Lucius's warning, Basalom leaped onto the slidewalk to close the gap before Avery could pull his weapon, but the distance was too great. Avery lunged for his pocket, there was a sound of tearing cloth, and he held a laser in his hand.

Pointed straight at Basalom.

''Basalom, is it?'' he said. ''I always wondered what you would name your mechanical lover.''

Lucius heard the icy tone in Avery's voice, knew what would happen next. He withdrew his eye from the wall, at the same time asking, *Friend Basalom, is your memory backed up?*

Not recently, I'm afraid, Basalom replied. *Pity. I've had some interesting insights in the past few days.*

Quickly; download your memory into me!

No time, Basalom replied, and Lucius, sticking his whole head out through the doorway, saw that he was correct. Avery's thumb was beginning to depress the laser's trigger button. Lucius could see the skin deforming. The button was beginning to slide. . . .

''No!''

Avery jerked at the sudden, overly amplified sound, and the beam went wide, slicing off Basalom's left arm. The arm landed with a thud on non-moving pavement; Basalom and Avery continued to slide away. The laser beam winked out as Avery looked to see who had shouted. Lucius stepped out into the corridor and said, "Do not harm Basalom. He is a thinking being, with just as much right to live as you."

Basalom made a move toward Avery, but Avery brought the laser around to bear on him again. "Wrong," Avery said. "He's a robot. Nothing more." Once again, his thumb began to depress the firing button.

Lucius's mind was awhirl in conflict. Yes, Basalom was certainly a robot, but couldn't he also be more? Couldn't he also be human, just as Lucius suspected he and his brethren were? Could he stand by and watch one human kill another simply because one was biological and the other was not?

The First Law said he couldn't. Zeroth Law implications further dictated that he must protect the more valuable of the two humans, if only one could be saved. Clearly, Basalom was the more valuable of the two, but how could Lucius save him?

Avery himself provided the answer. In the only similar instance of Zeroth-Law application Lucius had witnessed to date, Avery had demonstrated that it was right even to inflict injury to one human to avoid injury to the more valuable one. Lucius saw the possibility, saw that he *could* save Basalom's life, and he could even do so without killing Avery. It would still mean a First Law violation, but not a fatal one.

Not for Avery, at any rate, but Lucius didn't know what the conflict would eventually do to himself. If he and Basalom *weren't* human, he would be in direct violation of the First Law. Without justification, that would probably be enough to overload his brain with conflicting potentials.

Lucius hesitated a microsecond, but the other side of the argument was just as deadly. If Basalom *were* human, then not saving him would be an even worse violation of the law.

He felt a strange potential coursing through his circuits, the same potential he had noted earlier in connection with Avery. He cursed the biological fool before him for forcing him into this dilemma. He, Lucius, could very likely die in the attempt to save someone else.

There was no time to think it through any further. Avery's finger was dangerously close to triggering the laser again. In desperation, Lucius did the only thing he could think of to do: he drew back his arm to throw, formed his hand into a thin blade that would cause the least amount of pain possible, and flung it at Avery's outstretched arm.

In the moment it took the projectile to reach its target, Lucius wondered if he could have simply knocked the laser from Avery's hand, but it was easy to convince himself that he couldn't. It presented a much smaller target, most of which Avery's fingers covered anyway, and fingers would be even more difficult to reattach than would a forearm.

Besides, there was a certain amount of poetic justice in taking an entire limb.

Avery stared at the stump of his wrist in astonished disbelief. One moment a hand had been there, and the next moment it hadn't. He had hardly felt the pain when—whatever it was—cut it off; shock kept him from feeling it now.

Intelligence made him grasp the wrist in his left hand and squeeze until he'd closed off the arteries. He carefully avoided looking down at the slidewalk.

Slidewalk he thought dizzily. Yes, he'd best watch his footing, hadn't he? Blood could be slippery.

Dimly, through the tight focus his injury demanded of his attention, he was aware of shouting voices and the sound of footsteps. Someone shoved a hand under his arm and drew him erect; he hadn't been aware he was slumping to his knees. He looked up to see Janet's humaniform robot supporting him, heard it say, "Master Avery, we must get you to a hospital."

"No kidding," he managed to say through clenched teeth. It was beginning to hurt now.

Someone else shouted, "Lucius, come back here! Mandelbrot, stop him!" Metallic feet pounded away down the corridor.

Another pair of hands reached out to hold him, these ones warm and human, and he found himself looking into Janet's whitened face. She looked worse than he felt. "I'm sorry," she whispered. "Oh Wendell, I'm sorry."

"I am too," he said automatically, and was surprised to realize the words were true, but about what he had no idea.

The computer's voice woke Derec out of a sound sleep. "Master Derec, wake up. Master Derec."

"Mmmm?" was all he could manage at first. After the elation of figuring out his mother's name had faded, he'd realized how long he'd been without sleep and he had ordered a bed made for him right there in the study. He'd hoped that his new discovery would trigger memories of his past, and he'd supposed that sleeping on it would be the best way to integrate that knowledge into whatever subconscious switching network controlled memory, but now, even in his groggy state, he knew it hadn't worked. He suspected he'd slept *too* soundly for that. He'd been out before his head hit the pillow, exhausted, and he didn't feel any different now.

"Wake up," the computer said again. "Your father has been located."

That sped the waking process a bit. He sat up and shook his head, stood, and staggered over to the terminal. "Caffeine," he said as he sat down, and a moment later the desk delivered a cup of steaming black coffee. "Show me where he is," he said between gulps.

The screen lit to show Avery standing between two unfamiliar people. No, one should be familiar, Derec realized. That had to be his mother. Janet. Again he reached for the cascade of memories that should have been there, but nothing responded to the new stimulus.

That was her, though. It had to be. Then that other person wasn't a person at all, but her humaniform robot, the one Wolruf had chased northward from the lab. Evidently they had come back together this time. And brought Avery with them? That certainly seemed to be the case. Now that he looked, Derec could see that they were holding onto him, evidently making sure he didn't get away. Or was that—? No. Avery clutched his right wrist, and he had no hand below it. They were supporting him; that was it. But none of the three was doing anything about his injury! They were instead watching something out of the monitor's view to the right.

"Pan right," Derec ordered, and the view slid left in the screen. As it panned he saw Ariel standing in the doorway of what Derec could now see was indeed the lab where he'd revived the robots, and she was also looking intently down the corridor.

The objects of their attention slid into view: four robots—Mandelbrot, Adam, Eve, and Lucius—locked in battle.

They were a blur of motion. It was hard to tell who was on which side—hard even to tell who was *who* amid the constantly shifting shapes. Only Mandelbrot remained the same from moment to moment. At first it seemed that he fought against the other three, struggling to hold them all captive while they twisted and flowed out of his grasp, but it gradually became apparent that he and two of the others were all three trying to contain only one robot.

"Give me sound," Derec said, and suddenly his study

echoed with screeches and thuds and a peculiar ripping noise that Derec realized was the sound of robot cells being torn free like Velcro fasteners. The robots had changed tactics now; instead of trying to contain their captive—a task as impossible as stopping a flood with their hands—they began tearing him apart. Mandelbrot was doing the most damage. His rigid left arm moved like a piston, his hand pulling free chunks of silvery robot and flinging them away to splash against the walls and ceiling. The other two robots took over the job of flailing at the constantly shifting amoeba their captive had become, pulling off its arms when it tried to grow around them and forcing it back toward Mandelbrot and destruction.

At last Mandelbrot exposed his target: the robot's egg-shaped microfusion power pack. When he wrenched that free, the struggle instantly ceased. He backed away with the power pack in his hand, and the other two robots flowed back into their normal shapes: Adam the werewolf and Eve the silvery copy of Ariel. The third robot remained a much-diminished, ragged-edged tangle of appendages on the floor. It had undoubtedly been Lucius they'd destroyed. Somehow that didn't surprise Derec.

Then the implications of what he had seen soaked in, and he spilled coffee all over his desk. Swearing, but not at the spill, he leaped to his feet, knocking over his chair in his haste, and ran from the apartment. His father was hurt. His mother had come out of hiding. And there could only be one reason for the battle he had just witnessed: Lucius had injured a human being. He had directly violated the First Law of Robotics.

Wolruf was talking with the wolf when she felt the forest shudder beneath her feet.

"What I want to know," she'd been in the process of saying, "is whether or not your desire to serve 'umans is stronger in the immediate case, or over the long term. Do you think ahead to w'at your 'elp might do to your masters' civilization, or do you just follow your laws case by—what was that?''

The wolf had flinched, too, just as the forest had seemed to do. Now it said, "Involuntary response. A robot has just injured a human."

"W'at?" Wolruf felt her hackles rise. That was supposed to be impossible.

The wolf looked into the forest and spoke as if echoing a news broadcast, as it probably was. "The robot Lucius has inflicted non-fatal damage to the human Wendell Avery. Lucius has been deactivated, but all units are alerted to watch for aberrant behavior among other robots. All units must run a diagnostic self-check immediately." The wolf turned its head to look up at Wolruf. "I must comply," it said, and it froze like a statue.

Wolruf glanced around at the forest, wondering if she should use the opportunity to make her escape. Of all the times to be out in the forest with a robotic wolf, this was probably the worst. If some rogue idea were circulating around, some new thought that could actually allow a robot to override the Three Laws, then Wolruf couldn't think of a much worse place to run afoul of it than here with a robot who had already convinced itself that injuring animals was all right.

She forced herself to stay put. It had been Lucius and Avery involved, not this robot before her. Wolruf had lived around robots long enough to know that they seldom—if ever—did anything without a reason, and if ever a robot had a reason to harm a human, Lucius was the one. Scary as the precedent might be, the wolf didn't have a motive. No matter how much she worried about the long-term damage robots could do to a civilization, Wolruf didn't think she was in any danger now.

She waited impatiently for the wolf robot's consciousness to come back on line, in the meantime listening to the occasional chirps and cries of the forest's real occupants. Quite a few of them were genuine, by the sound of it. Quite a few of the plants were, too. The fresh, clean aroma of growing things was a constant delight to a nose too often idle in the city.

That was a good argument in favor of robots right there, Wolruf realized. They had repaired a planet-wide ecosystem in only a few months, with much more careful attention to detail than she or her entire society could achieve. Wolruf's home world needed such attention, and soon. Most of the forests there were already gone, as were the wide open spaces and the clean lakes. Centuries of industrialization had left scars that would probably never heal on their own. Even accounting for the difficulties inherent in working around an existing population, robots would probably be able to repair it all in a few years, or decades at the longest.

There was no denying that robots would be useful if she took them home with her. But that still didn't tell her whether or not they would also be harmful.

She was no closer to an answer than before. And now she had to worry about the possibility of immediate danger as well as long-term effects of using robots.

The wolf returned to life as quickly as it had frozen. "My functions check out marginal," it said. "I am not a direct threat to humans, but under the current conditions my ability to kill animals has caused some alarm. I have been instructed to return to the city for deeper evaluation."

"Oh," Wolruf said.

"If you wish to accompany me, we can continue our discussion on the way."

"All right."

"You were asking about the city's consideration for long-range effects of its actions." The robot led off through the ferns toward a large boulder, which obligingly grew a door for them when they were still a few paces away. "I have accessed the pertinent operation guidelines from Central, and find that very little long-term planning exists. However, since this was an experimental city built primarily to test the physical function of the cellular robot concept, that lack of guidelines may not be pertinent to the question. It seems likely that under actual implementation conditions, whatever long-range goals the city's inhabitants had for themselves would be included in the city programming."

They stepped into the elevator and turned around to watch the door slide closed, cutting off the sights and sounds and smells of forest once again. They began to descend, and Wolruf turned her attention to what the robot had said. She had to wade through the unfamiliar terms in its speech to get its meaning, but she was getting good at gathering sense from context. The robot had just said that long-term goals were the responsibility of the humans being served. Which, to answer her question, meant no, the robots wouldn't concern themselves with it because they believed it was already being covered.

Wolruf laughed aloud. When the robot asked her to explain, she said, "You've 'eard the cliché about the blind leading the blind?"

"No, but I have accessed the appropriate files. I fail to see the application here."

Wolruf laughed again. " 'umans, at least my particular breed of them—and to all appearances Derec's breed as well—don't pay much more attention to long-term problems than you do."

"Oh," the wolf said. "We will have to take this under consideration."

The elevator came to a stop and the doors opened onto the underground city. Wolruf stepped out ahead of the robot. "Good," she said. "I was 'oping you'd say that."

• • •

The city built the hospital in the suite of rooms just down the corridor from the lab. Medical robots arrived while it was still differentiating, took Avery inside, and made quick work of preparing his wound for surgery. The operating room grew around them while they cleaned the wound, and within minutes they had him anesthetized and were hard at work grafting his hand back on.

Ariel watched in morbid fascination from behind the sterile room's transparent wall. To her left stood Derec's mother and her companion robot, to her right Adam and Eve and Mandelbrot. The robots were watching the operation with the same fascination as Ariel, but Derec's mother was watching Ariel as much as anything else.

"You're David's lover, aren't you?" she finally asked, her tone less than approving. It was the first thing either of them had said to the other.

"That's right," Ariel said without looking away from the window. Where did this woman get off? she wondered. No introduction, no apology, just "You're David's lover." She didn't know a thing about the situation, yet she still acted as if she were in control. Ariel turned her head enough to address the reflection beside her own in the window and said, "His name is Derec now."

"I heard. I've never liked it. It sounds like a spacesuit manufacturer."

"Exactly," Ariel said around a smile.

"Why did he change it?"

"Long story."

"I see."

The medical robots were using some sort of glue on hold the ends of bone together. Lucius's weapon had been sharp and moving fast; the severed edges were smooth and easily repaired. He had probably done that on purpose, Ariel realized. She wondered why he had bothered. She watched the robots spread the glue on either end, press the two together, and hold them rigid until the glue set. She hoped they'd checked to make sure it was aligned properly; something about the glue looked permanent.

"You're not worth the effort he's put in on finding you," Ariel said suddenly.

"What?"

"You heard me. As soon as he hears about this, Derec is going to come running in here all ready for a big reconciliation. He wants his family back, and he'll take what he gets, but you're no prize. Neither of you. You two are living proof that scientists shouldn't have children."

"I suppose you're an expert on the subject."

"I know how to treat one."

"How could you? You don't— Do you?" The woman was clearly horrified at the thought.

"What's the matter, don't like the idea of being a grandmother?" Ariel snorted. "Relax, you're safe. *He* took care of it for you." She tilted her head toward the window. "One of his wonderful experiments ran amok and killed the fetus while it was still only a few weeks old."

"You sound as if you hold *me* responsible."

"You ran off and left your son in the hands of a lunatic. What am I supposed to think?"

"I couldn't take him with me. I—I needed to be alone."

"You should have thought about that before you had him." Ariel looked directly at Derec's mother for the first time since they had begun speaking to one another. If she had looked earlier she might have held her tongue; the woman's skin was gray, and she looked as if she had aged twenty years in the last few minutes.

Her robot was growing concerned, too. It said, "Mistress Janet, Mistress Ariel, I don't believe this conversation should continue."

Janet. That was her name. Ariel had been struggling for it since she'd first seen her.

Janet said, "It's all right, Basalom. Ariel isn't telling me anything I didn't already know." She smiled a fleeting smile. "I've had plenty of time to dwell on my mistakes." Looking back through the window at Avery and the medical robots, she said, "We thought having a child might save our marriage. Can you imagine anything sillier? People who don't get along in the first place certainly aren't going to get along any better under the stress of having a child, but we didn't see that then. We just knew we were falling out of love, and we tried the only thing we could think of to stop it from happening."

Ariel felt herself blush guiltily at Janet's admission. She'd been thinking along similar lines herself just yesterday, hadn't she? She hadn't actually come out and said that a baby would bring her and Derec closer together again, but she'd been working toward that concept. Was it so surprising, then, to find that Derec's parents had done the same thing?

"Treating the symptoms doesn't often cure the disease," Ariel said, her tone considerably softer than before. "I guess you should have looked for the reason why you were falling out of love in the first place."

"I know that now."

More softly still, Ariel asked, "Why do you think you did fall out of love?"

Janet's laugh was a derisive "Ha!" She nodded at Avery as Ariel had done earlier. "He was out to transform the galaxy; I wanted to study it first. He wanted a castle for everyone and a hundred robots in every castle, but I wanted to preserve a little diversity in the universe. I was more interested in the nature of intelligence and the effect of environment on its development, while he was more interested in using intelligence to modify the environment to suit it. We argued about it all the time. Small wonder we started to hate each other.''

Derec spared Ariel from having to reply to that. He burst into the room at a dead run, skidded to a stop just in time to avoid crashing into the windowed wall, and demanded of anyone who would answer, ''What did you do with Lucius's body?''

CHAPTER 7
THE THUD OF
ONE DROPPED SHOE

Janet could hardly believe her ears. "What kind of a way is that to greet someone you haven't seen in years?"

Derec looked properly sheepish. He also looked as if he'd slept in his clothing and hadn't bothered to look in a mirror before he'd left the apartment. One lock of hair stuck straight out from his right temple.

"Sorry," he said. "Hello, Mother. I've missed you. How's Dad?" He looked through the window, but before Janet could answer him he lost his sheepish look and said, "Looks like he'll live. But without a power pack Lucius won't last more than an hour or so. I've got to get enough power to his brain to keep him going or we'll lose the chance to find out what made him do this."

Janet couldn't suppress a grin. He sounded just like his father. Or maybe like herself, she admitted, if she'd been thinking a little more clearly.

Ariel wasn't as amused. "Robots, robots, robots! Is that all you can think about?" she nearly screamed at him. "There's more to life than robots!"

Derec shook his head, but Janet could see the determination in his eyes. "No, that's not all I think about. It's just that this happens to be about the most important thing to happen in the entire history of robotics. If we lose this chance to study it, we may never get another."

"Derec's right," Janet said. "If I hadn't been so rattled I'd have thought of it myself. Basalom, where—"

The robot at Ariel's side interrupted. "I do not think it would be wise to revive him. He is dangerous."

"I agree with Mandelbrot," the wolflike learning machine beside him said. "Much as we regret the loss of our companion, his experiences have damaged him beyond repair. It would be best to let his pathways randomize."

Janet looked at the old, Ferrier-model robot. Mandelbrot? She'd thought she'd heard that name shouted earlier. Could this be the one? It seemed impossible, but he *did* have a dianite arm. . . .

"Maybe so," Derec said, "but not until I get a recording of them first. Now where is his body?"

"In the lab next door," said Mandelbrot.

"Great." Derec turned to go, but stopped and looked at Janet again. "I, uh, could probably use your help if you want to come along."

She felt the tension in the room ease slightly. She looked from him to Ariel to Wendell in the operating room, wondering if she should go. She didn't want to leave Wendell, but the medical robot had given him a general anesthetic in order to stop him from thinking about his injury, so it really made no difference to him. Going with Derec, on the other hand, might matter to *him*. A little stunned that she might actually care about what either of them felt, or that she might feel something herself, she said, "I don't think I'm doing anyone any good here, so sure, why not?"

"I'll stay here," Ariel said.

Janet couldn't tell if she meant that angrily or helpfully. She didn't suppose it mattered much; the same response would work for either case. "Thank you," she said, and let Derec lead her from the room.

Basalom followed along, as did the two learning machines. They found the remains of the third, Lucius, resting like a battered starfish on the floor just inside the door to the lab. It looked as if part of the battle had gone on in there as well, but Derec, stepping over Lucius's body, said, "I guess I forgot to clean up. Central, fix these exam tables, please. And go ahead and reabsorb the loose cells on the floor. All but what belongs to Lucius, of course."

The sandy grit surrounding the pedestals on the floor sank into the surface, and the pedestals simultaneously grew taller and spread out at the top to form three separate exam tables. Janet nodded to Basalom and said, "Go ahead and put him on one. Then go out and scrape up what you can from outside."

Basalom lifted Lucius easily with his one remaining hand and deposited him on the middle table, then left the room. The Ariel-shaped learning machine went with him. Janet was itching to speak with one of the learning machines, but she supposed there would be time for that later. She was itching to speak with Derec as well, but he was already absorbed in the task of hooking up a variable power supply and a brain activity monitor to Lucius.

She supposed she could be helping with that, at least. She walked over to stand across the exam table from him and said, "Plus and minus five volts will do for his memories. If you hold it at that, he shouldn't wake up, and even if he does, he'll still be immobilized because the body cells take twenty volts before they can move."

Derec nodded. The stray hair at his temple waved like a tree limb in a breeze. "Good," he said. "Any special place I should attach the leads? The few times I've worked on these guys, I've just stuck stuff anywhere and let the cells sort it out, but I wasn't sure if that was the best way."

Janet couldn't resist reaching out and brushing his hair down. He looked surprised at first, then smiled when he realized what she was doing.

"Anywhere is fine," she said. "When I designed the cells, I gave them enough hard wiring to figure out what to do with all the various types of input they were likely to get."

"Good."

She watched Derec clip the power supply's three leads to the ends of three different arms, then turn up the voltage to five. He then took the brain monitor's headphone-shaped sensor and moved it over the robot's unconventional body, searching for its positronic brain. The monitor began to beep when he reached the base of one of the arms, and he wedged it in place with one pickup underneath and one on top.

The monitor flickered with sharp-edged waveforms, hundreds of them joining to fill the screen until it was a jumble of multicolored lines. "Looks like we caught him in time," Derec said. "There seems to be quite a bit of mental activity." He reached up and switched in a filter, and the jumble diminished to a manageable half-dozen or so waveforms. They weren't actual voltage traces, but rather representations of activity in the various levels of the brain, useful for visualizing certain types of thoughts.

Janet frowned. "Are those supposed to be the Three Laws?"

"That's right."

The pattern was still recognizable as the one built into every positronic brain at the time of manufacture—but just barely. Each of the laws showed in a separate hue of green, but overlaying them all were two companion waves, a deep violet one that split and rejoined much as the Three Laws did, and a lighter blue one weaving in and out around the laws and linking up with other signals from all over the screen. The effect looked as if the violet and blue waves were purposefully entangling the laws, preventing them from altering their potential beyond carefully delineated levels. Janet suspected that was just what they were doing. Visual analogy didn't always work in describing a robot's inner workings, but in this case it looked pretty straightforward.

"I'd say that explains a lot," she said.

Derec flipped to another band, following the two waves as they wove from the Three Laws through the self-awareness section and into the duty queue. "Looks like he's built a pretty heavy web of rationalization around just about all the pre-defined areas of thought," he said. "Normal diagnostic procedure would be to wake him up and ask him what all that means, but I don't think we want to do that just yet. Adam, you know how he thinks; can you make sense of it?"

The one remaining learning machine stepped over to Derec's side. Adam? Had he known the significance of that name when he chose it, or had it been given to him? Janet supposed the other one would be Eve, then. And this one, the renegade, was Lucius. Why hadn't he gone for the obvious and called himself Lucifer? She itched to ask them. She *had* to talk with them soon.

In answer to Derec's question, Adam said, "The violet potential schematic corresponds to the Laws of Humanics. The blue one is the Zeroth Law of Robotics."

"Beg your pardon?" Janet asked. "Laws of Humanics? Zeroth Law? What are you talking about?"

Her learning machine looked over at her and said, "We have attempted to develop a set of laws governing human behavior, laws similar to the ones that govern our own. They are, of course, purely descriptive rather than compulsory, but we felt that understanding them might give us an understanding of human behavior which we otherwise lacked. As for the Zeroth Law, we felt that the Three Laws were insufficient in defining our obligations toward the human race in general, so we attempted to define that obligation ourselves.''

Janet was careful not to express the joy she felt, for fear of influencing the robot somehow, but inside she was ecstatic. This was perfect! Her experiment was working out after all. Her learning machines had begun to generalize from their experiences. ''And what did you come up with?'' she asked.

''Bear in mind that these laws describe potential conditions within a positronic brain, so words are inadequate to describe them perfectly; however, they can be expressed approximately as follows. The First Law of Humanics: All beings will do that which pleases them most. The Second Law of Humanics: A sentient being may not harm a friend, or through inaction allow a friend to come to harm. The Third Law of Humanics: A sentient being will do what a friend asks, but a friend may not ask unreasonable things.'' He paused, perhaps giving Janet time to assimilate the new laws' meanings.

Not bad. Not bad at all. Like he'd said, they certainly weren't compulsory as far as most humans went, but Janet doubted she could have done any better. ''And what is your Zeroth Law?'' she asked.

''That is much more difficult to state in words, but a close approximation would be that any action should serve the greatest number of humans possible.'' Adam nodded toward Lucius. ''Lucius has taken the Law a step farther than Eve or I, and we believe it was that step which led him to do what he did to Dr. Avery. He believes that the value of the humans in question should also be considered.''

Eve. She'd guessed right. ''And you don't?''

Adam raised his arms with the palms of his hands up. It took Janet a moment to recognize it as a shrug, since she'd never seen a robot use the gesture before. Adam said, ''I am . . . uncomfortable with the subjectivity of the process. I had hoped to find a more definite operating principle."

"But Lucius is satisfied with it."

"That seems to be the case."

"Why do you suppose he is and you aren't?"

"Because," Adam said, again hesitating. "Because he believes himself to be human."

If the robot were hoping to shock her with that revelation, he was going to be disappointed. Janet had expected something like this would happen from the start; indeed, in a way it was the whole point of the experiment. She waited patiently for the question she knew was coming.

Adam didn't disappoint her. He looked straight into her eyes with his own metallic ones and said, "Each of us has struggled with this question since we awakened, but none of us have been able to answer it to our mutual satisfaction. You created us, though. Please tell us: are we human?"

Janet used the same palms-up gesture Adam had used. "I don't know. You tell me."

Adam knew the sudden surge of conflicting potentials for what it was: frustration. He had experienced enough of it in his short life to recognize it when it happened. This time the frustration came from believing his search for truth was over and suddenly finding that it wasn't.

He felt a brief Second Law urge to answer her question with a simple declarative statement, but he shunted that aside easily. She obviously wanted more than that, and so did he. She wanted to see the reasoning behind his position; he wanted to see if that reasoning would withstand her scrutiny.

He opened a comlink channel to Eve and explained the situation to her. Together they tried to establish a link with Lucius, but evidently the five volts Derec was supplying him hadn't been enough to wake him. They would have to do without his input. Adam wasn't all that disappointed; Lucius's reasoning had led him to violate the First Law.

Janet was waiting for Adam's response. Carefully, consulting with Eve at every turn, he began to outline the logic that had led them to their conclusion that any intelligent organic being had to be considered human. He began with his own awakening on Tau Puppis IV and proceeded through the incident with the Ceremyons, through Lucius's experiments in creating human beings in Robot City, through the robots' return to Tau Puppis and their dealings with the Kin, to their final encounter with Aranimas. He explained how each encounter with an alien being reinforced the robots' belief that body shape made no difference in the essential humanity of the mind inside it, and how those same contacts had even made differences in intelligence and technological advancement seem of questionable importance.

Throughout his presentation, Adam tried to judge Janet's reaction to it by her facial expression, but she was giving nothing away. She merely nodded on occasion and said, "I'm with you so far."

At last he reached the concept of Vitalism, the belief that organic beings were somehow inherently superior to electromechanical ones, and how the robots could find no proof of its validity. He ended with, "That lack of proof led Lucius to conclude that Vitalism is false, and that robots could therefore be considered human. Neither Eve nor I—nor Mandelbrot, for that matter—were able to convince ourselves of this, and now that Lucius's belief has led him into injuring a human, we feel even less comfortable with it. We don't know what to believe."

Adam waited for her response. Surely she would answer him now, after he had laid out the logic for her so meticulously.

His frustration level rose to a new height, however, when

she merely smiled an enigmatic smile and said, "I'm sure you'll figure it out."

Derec felt just as frustrated as Adam. He had hoped that finding his mother would knock loose some memories from his amnesic brain, but so far nothing had come of the encounter except a vague sense of familiarity that could be easily attributed to her similarity to Avery.

She seemed just like him in many ways. He was a competent roboticist, and so was she. Avery never divulged information to anyone if he could help it, and evidently neither did she. Avery was always testing someone, and here she stood, leading poor Adam on when it was obvious she didn't know the answer to his question either.

He glanced up at the monitor, checking to see if the signal was any clearer. While Janet and Adam had been talking, he had been trying to trace another unfamiliar potential pattern in Lucius's brain, this one an indistinct yellow glow surrounding an entire level of activity, but the monitor's trace circuitry couldn't isolate the thought it represented. Whatever it was, it fit none of the standard robotic thought patterns.

He heard Janet say, "I'm sure you'll figure it out," and took that as his cue. "Adam, maybe you can help me figure *this* out. What's that pattern represent?"

Adam looked up to the monitor. "I do not recognize it," he said.

"Can you copy it and tell me what it does?"

"I do not wish to contaminate my mind with Lucius's thought patterns."

"Put it in temporary storage, then."

Adam looked as if he would protest further, but either the Second Law of Robotics or his belief that Derec would follow the Third Law of Humanics made him obey instead.

He fixed his gaze on the monitor for a moment, then looked away, toward the wall.

Derec wondered what was so interesting all of a sudden about the wall. Adam didn't seem inclined to clue him in, either; he merely stood there, hands clenching and un-clenching.

Then Derec realized what was *behind* the wall. Just on the other side was the hospital where Avery was still undergoing surgery.

"Erase that pattern," he commanded, and Adam relaxed. "What was it?"

Adam turned to face Derec and Janet again. "It was a potential like those I have come to associate with emotions," he said. "However, I have not felt this one before. It was an unspecified negative bias on all thoughts concerning Dr. Avery."

Derec glanced over at Janet, saw that she wore an expression of triumph.

Adam saw it, too. "How can you approve?" he asked. "I have never felt this emotion, but I know what it had to be. Lucius was angry. Considering the degree of bias and the ultimate influence it had upon his actions, I would say he was furious."

"What's one thing a human can do that a robot can't?" Janet asked in return.

"You wish me to say, 'feel emotion,'" said Adam, "but that is incorrect. Every robot experiences a degree of po-tential bias on various subjects. If you wish to call it emo-tion, you may, but it is merely the result of experience strengthening certain positronic pathways in the brain at the expense of others."

"And everything you know comes from experience, doesn't it?"

"Nearly everything, yes."

"So?"

Derec could see where her argument was leading. "A *tabula rasa!*" he exclaimed. He saw instant comprehension written in Janet's smile, but Adam remained unmoved. Derec said, "'*Tabula rasa*' means 'blank slate.'" It's a metaphor for the way the human mind supposedly starts out before experience begins carving a personality into it. That's one side of the Nature-versus-Nurture argument for the development of consciousness. Dad told me about that just a couple weeks ago, but he was talking about erasing the city Central on the Kin's planet, and I didn't make the connection." He looked back at his mother. "That's what you were trying to prove with Adam and Eve and Lucius, wasn't it? You were trying to prove that the *tabula rasa* argument is valid."

"Guilty," she said.

"You were *trying* to produce human minds?" Adam asked.

Janet looked as if she wouldn't answer, but after a moment she sighed and said, "Ah, what the heck. Looks like that aspect of the experiment's over anyway. Yeah, that's one of the things I was trying to do. I was trying to create intelligence. I gave you what I consider the bare minimum in a robot: curiosity and the Three Laws, and I turned you loose to see if any of you would become anything more. Of course I didn't count on you all getting together, but that doesn't seem to have hurt anything. You've all surpassed anything I expected. Welcome to the human race." She held out her hand.

Adam reached out gingerly, as if after all this time spent searching for the truth, he was now unsure he wanted the honor she conveyed. He took her hand in his and shook it gently, and still holding on, he asked, "What about Basalom?"

Janet shook her head. "The jury's still out on him. I think

I gave him too much initial programming for him to develop a human personality.''

"But you're not sure?"

"No, I'm not sure. Why?"

"Because if *you're* not sure, then neither could Lucius be, and he was right in protecting Basalom's life.''

Derec had to admit that Adam's argument made sense. So why were the hackles standing up on the back of his neck? He looked back to the monitor, saw the fuzzy yellow glow that Adam said indicated anger. That was why. With only five volts going to his brain, Lucius was effectively in suspended animation at the moment. He was still furious at Avery, and if they woke him up, he might very well continue to be furious. If they were going to reanimate Frankenstein's monster, Derec wanted to calm him down first, at least. If possible, he wanted to do even more.

"What can we do to make sure it doesn't happen again?" he asked aloud.

"Treat him better," Janet said. "Follow the Laws of Humanics they've set up for us.''

Derec couldn't suppress a sardonic laugh. "That may be fine for us, but what about Dad? He's not going to do anything he doesn't want to.''

His mother tossed her head, flinging her blond hair back over her shoulders. "Leave your father to me," she said.

Avery woke from the anesthetic with the impression that his tongue had swollen to twice its normal size. He tried to swallow, but his mouth was too dry for that. His vision was blurry, too, and when he tried to raise his right hand to rub his eyes, it didn't respond.

He was in bad shape, that much was clear. Damn that meddlesome robot! Damn him and damn Janet for building him.

He was evidently sitting up in bed, judging from the few

somatic clues he could gather. He opened his mouth and used his swollen tongue and dry mouth to croak out the single word: "Water."

He heard a soft clink of glassware, the blessed wet gurgle of liquid being poured, and then a dark shape leaned over him and held the glass to his lips. He sipped at it, blinking his eyes as he did in an effort to clear them so he could see his benefactor.

She spoke and saved him the effort of identification. "Well, Wendy, it looks like we have a lot to talk about, and finally plenty of time to do it in."

Turning his head away from the glass, he said, "We have nothing to discuss." It came out more like, "We a uthi oo ithcuth."

She understood him anyway. "Ah, well, yes we do. There's us, for instance. I can't really believe it's just co-incidence that brought us back together after all this time."

Avery blinked a few more times, and his vision finally began to clear. Janet was sitting on a stool beside his bed, wearing a soft, light blue bodysuit with a zippered neck, which she'd pulled strategically low. *Watch yourself,* he thought as his eyes immediately strayed to the target she'd provided.

She smiled, no doubt recognizing her slight victory.

"I don' know wha' you're talking abou'," he said carefully.

Her smile never wavered. "I think you do." She held the glass to his lips and let him drink again while she said, "Face it; this whole city project of yours seems almost designed to attract my attention. You didn't really think I'd ignore it once I heard about it, did you?"

Avery's tongue seemed to be returning to normal. When Janet removed the glass, he said, "I tried not to think about you at all."

"Didn't work, did it? I tried the same thing."

Her question made him distinctly uncomfortable. "What do you want from me?" he demanded. "I'm not going to take you back, if that's it."

"I didn't ask that," she said, frowning.

"What, then?"

Janet set the glass down. "Ah, Wendy. Always business. All right, then, we'll start with my learning machines. I want you to leave them alone."

"I told you I would before you had Lucius attack me. I'll be glad to be rid of them."

"I didn't have Lucius attack you. He decided to do it on his own. Considering the provocation, I think he showed admirable restraint."

"He injured a human to protect a robot. You call that restraint?" Avery looked down to his right hand, found the reason why it didn't respond. It was encased in a sleeve of dianite from his elbow to the ends of his fingers. Tiny points of light winked on and off along its length, each one above a recessed slide control. No doubt tiny robot cells were busy inside his arm as well, repairing the damage Lucius had done.

"He injured a human to protect another human," Janet said. "Or so he thought. Evidently that's a trick you taught him."

"Another of my many mistakes."

Janet laughed. "My, how times do change us. The Wendell Avery I knew could no more have admitted a mistake than he could fly."

"And the Janet Anastasi I knew could no more have cared about a robot than she did about her son."

She blushed; he had scored a hit. She didn't back away, though. "Let's talk about David for a minute," she said. "You wiped his mind after I left. Care to tell me why?"

Avery looked around for the medical robot, thinking maybe he could claim fatigue and get it to usher Janet out, but there was no robot in sight. No doubt she had given it some line of rationalization to convince it to leave them alone. He wished he'd had the forethought to hide a Key to Perihelion in his pockets; he'd have gladly taken his chances with the teleportation device rather than face any more of Janet's questions. It looked like he was going to have to, though. She didn't look like she was prepared to let him off the hook just yet.

Sighing in defeat, he said, "I wish I could tell you. I . . . went a little crazy there for a while, I'm afraid. He says I told him it was a test to see if he was worthy of inheriting my cities, but whether that was really it, or if I had a different reason, I don't know."

"You don't suppose you could have been trying to eliminate his memory of *me*, do you?"

Avery shrugged. "I have no idea. Possibly. I was quite . . . angry with you."

"Ah, yes, anger. It makes people do things they later regret. We'll return to that in a minute, but let's not change the subject again just yet. You and David had pretty much patched things up again, hadn't you? You were getting along pretty well. Almost like a normal father and son. What happened to that?"

"He betrayed my trust," Avery said. His voice came out harsh, and he held out his left hand for more water.

Pouring, Janet asked, "Betrayed how? What did he do?"

Avery accepted the glass and drank half of its contents in two gulps. "He turned my city into a zoo, that's what. Worse, he turned it into a caricature of a zoo. Behind my back."

Janet's laugh was pure derision. "You were ready to sacrifice everything you'd gained with him because of that?"

"It wasn't the act itself, but the betrayal."

"Which you can't bring yourself to forgive. Not even

after all you did to him, and all the forgiving he had to do.''

Avery gulped down the rest of his water. He had no answer for her. He was thinking of all the times in the last few weeks he had tried to open up to Derec, tried to make up for his earlier failings as a father. At the time it had seemed the most difficult thing he'd ever done, which was why the sudden discovery of Derec's subterfuge had affected him the way it had.

Janet got up off her stool and stood beside the bed, looking down on him with angry eyes. ''I wouldn't come back to you even if you'd have me. Why do you think I left you in the first place? Because you could never forgive anything, that's why. The least little mistake and you'd be sore for a week, and Frost help me if I made a big one. Is it any wonder I learned to prefer the company of robots?'' She turned away and stalked to the window separating the recovery room from the rest of the hospital. Beyond it, Derec and Ariel were discussing something with the medical robot. Janet said, ''You've learned to admit to your own mistakes; isn't it time you learned to forgive other people for theirs?''

''Is that what you want from me, then? You want me to forgive our son for his . . . mistake?''

Janet turned back to face him. ''That's right, I want you to forgive him. I don't think he even made a mistake, but that's beside the point. The practice will do you good, because when you're done forgiving David, then I want you to forgive Lucius for what he did, too.''

Avery looked for signs of a joke, but she seemed to be serious. He snorted. ''You don't 'forgive' robots. You melt them down and start over. Which is what I should have done with your three the moment I found them.''

''You'd have been committing murder if you had. In fact, according to David, you almost did just that. If he hadn't revived them, you'd have been guilty of that, too.''

"Janet, I think you've been away from human companionship a little too long. They're robots."

"They've got intelligent, inquisitive minds. They feel emotion. You know what was going on in Lucius's mind when he saw you again? He was mad. Furious, to hear Adam tell it. Does that sound like a robot to you?"

Avery waved his free arm. "Oh, they're accomplished mimics, granted. You did a wonderful job with them in that regard. But there's no way they can be anything but robots. They've got positronic brains, for God's sake. It's like—" He searched for an example as unlikely as a robot becoming human. "Ah, it's like Derec's precious ecosystem just over our heads. Most of the trees are robots. They do just about everything a tree can do, including feeding the birds, but could you seriously suggest that any of them really *are* trees? Nonsense. They're robots, just like your 'learning machines.' "

Janet sat back down on the stool and took the empty glass from Avery. "I think we're arguing semantics here. My robots may not be human in the most technical sense, but in every way that counts, they are. They're every bit as human as any of the aliens you've met, and you've granted human status to most of those."

"Reluctantly," Avery growled. He remembered an earlier thought and asked, "Was that what you were attempting to do? Create your own aliens?"

"I was trying to create a true intelligence of any sort. Alien, human, I didn't care. I just wanted to see what I'd get."

"And you think you've got both." Avery didn't make it a question. He ran a hand through his hair, then let out a long sigh. "I don't care. I'm tired. Call them what you want if it'll please you, but keep 'em away from me. As soon as this heals"—he nodded toward his right arm—"I'm leaving anyway, and you can do whatever you please."

Janet shook her head. "No, you're not going anywhere until we agree on a lot more than just my learning machines. I don't much like your cities, either."

"Fat lot you can do about that," Avery said.

Janet smiled sweetly, but her words were a dagger of ice. "Oh, well, as a matter of fact, there is. You see, I patented the entire concept, from the dianite cell all the way up, in my name."

CHAPTER 8
THE OTHER SHOE DROPS

The apartment was empty when Wolruf arrived. She padded softly through the living room, noting Ariel's book reader lying on the end table by her chair and the empty niche where Mandelbrot usually stood, then went into Derec's study and saw the bed there, still rumpled from sleep. The computer terminal was still on. She saw no cup in evidence, but the air conditioner hadn't quite removed the smell of spilled coffee.

"W'ere is everybody?" she asked of the room.

"Derec and Ariel's location is restricted," Central replied.

Oh, great. Now they'd all disappeared. Unless . . .

"Are they at the same restricted location as before?" she asked.

"That is correct."

Wolruf laughed aloud. She was learning how to deal with these pseudo-intelligences. She stopped in her own room just long enough to freshen up, then left the apartment and caught the slidewalk.

She found not only Derec and Ariel in the robotics lab,

but an unfamiliar woman who had to be Derec's mother as well. Derec was busy with the humaniform robot Wolruf had attempted to catch the last time she'd been near here. He was trying to remove the stump of its severed arm, and by his expression not having much success at it. Ariel was holding a light for him and Derec's mother was offering advice.

"Try reaching inside and feeling for it," she said.

Derec obediently reached in through the access hatch in the robot's chest, felt around inside for something, and jerked his hand out again in a hurry. "Ouch! There's still live voltage in there!"

"Not enough to hurt you," his mother said patiently. "Not when he's switched into standby mode like this. Would you like me to do it?"

"No, I'll get it." Derec reached inside again, but stopped when he heard Wolruf's laugh. He looked up and saw her in the doorway.

"'Ello."

"Hi." Grinning, Derec withdrew his hand from the robot and used it to gesture. "Mom, this is my friend Wolruf. Wolruf, this my mother, Janet Anastasi."

"Pleased to meet you," Wolruf said, stepping forward and holding out a hand.

Janet looked anything but pleased to be so suddenly confronted with an alien, but she swallowed gamely and took the proffered appendage. "Likewise," she said.

Wolruf gave her hand a squeeze and let go. Looking over Janet's shoulder, she noticed a huddle of four robots in the far corner of the lab: three learning machines and Mandelbrot. They looked to be in communications fugue. Nodding toward them, she said, "I 'eard Lucius 'urt Avery some'ow."

"That's right," Ariel said. "He was trying to protect Basalom, here. We've got him in psychotherapy, if you can call four robots in an argument psychotherapy. They're trying to convince him it's all right."

"It *is?*" Wolruf asked.

"Well, not the actual *act*," Derec said, "but the logic he used wasn't at fault. He just made a mistake, that's all. He thought he was protecting a human." Derec outlined the logic Lucius had used, including the First and Zeroth Law considerations that had finally made him do what he'd done.

Wolruf listened with growing concern. The Zeroth Law was just the thing she'd hoped for to reassure her that taking robots home with her wouldn't destroy her homeworld's society, but if that same law let a robot injure its master, then she didn't see how it could be a good thing.

"I don't know," she said. "Sounds like a bad tradeoff to me."

"How so?" Janet asked.

"I'm wondering 'ow *useful* all this is going to be. Right now I'm not sure about regular robots, much less ones who think they're 'uman."

"What aren't you sure about?"

Was Derec's mother just being polite, or did she really want to know? Wolruf wondered if this was the time to be getting into all this, to bring up the subject of her going home and to get into all her reasons for hesitating, but she supposed there really wasn't going to be a much better time. She knew what Derec and Ariel thought about the subject; maybe this Janet would have something new to say. "I'm not sure about taking any of these robots 'ome with me," Wolruf said. "I'm not sure about w'at they might decide to do on their own, and I'm not sure about w'at might 'appen to us even if they just follow orders."

"I don't understand."

"She's talking about protecting people from themselves," Ariel said.

"Am I?"

"Sure you are. I've been thinking about it, too. The problem with robot cities is that they're too responsive. Anything you want them to do, they'll do it, so long as it doesn't hurt anybody. The trouble is, they don't reject stupid ideas, and they don't think ahead."

"That's the people's job," Janet said.

"Just w'at one of the robots in the forest told me," Wolruf said. "Trouble is, people won't always do it. Or w'en they realize they made a mistake, it'll be too late."

Janet looked to Derec. "Pessimistic lot you run around with."

"They come by it honestly," he said, grinning. "We've been burned more than once by these cities. Just about every time, it's been something like what they're talking about. Taking things too literally, or not thinking them through."

"Isn't Central supposed to be doing that?"

"Central is really just there to coordinate things," Derec said. "It's just a big computer, not very adaptable." He looked down at Basalom again, nodded to Ariel to have her shine the light inside again as well, and peered inside the robot's shoulder. After a moment he found what he was looking for, reached gingerly inside, and grunted with the strain of pushing something stubborn aside. The something gave with a sudden click and the stump of the robot's arm popped off, trailing wires.

"There's also a committee of supervisory robots," Ariel said, "but they don't really do any long-range planning either. And they're all subject to the Three Laws, so anybody who wants to could order them to change something, and unless it clearly hurt someone else, they'd have to do it."

"No matter how stupid it was," Janet said.

"Right." Derec unplugged the wires between Basalom's upper arm and the rest of his body.

Janet looked thoughtful. "Hmmm," she said. "Sounds like what these cities all need is a mayor."

"Mayor?" Wolruf asked.

"Old human custom," Janet replied. "A mayor is a person in charge of a city. He or she is supposed to make decisions that affect the whole city and everyone in it. They're supposed to have the good of the people at heart, so ideally they make the best decisions they can for the largest number of people for the longest period of time."

"Ideally," Wolruf growled. "We know 'ow closely people follow ideals."

"People, sure." Janet waved a hand toward the four robots in the corner. "But how about dedicated idealists?"

Ariel was so startled she dropped the light. It clattered to the floor and went out, but by the time she bent down to retrieve it, it was glowing again, repaired.

"Something wrong, dear?" Janet asked her.

"You'd let one of *them* be in charge of a city?"

"Yes, I would."

"And you'd *live* there?"

"Sure. They're not dangerous."

"Not dangerous! Look at what—"

"Lucius made the right decision, as far as I'm concerned."

"Maybe," Ariel said. "What worries me is the thought process he went through to make it." She clicked off the light; Derec wasn't working on Basalom anymore anyway. He was staring at Ariel and Janet as if he'd never heard two people argue before. Ariel ignored his astonished look and said, "The greatest good for the greatest number of people. That could easily translate to 'the end justifies the means.' Are you seriously suggesting that's a viable operating principle?"

"We're not talking an Inquisition here," Janet said.

"But what if we were? What if the greatest good meant killing forty-nine percent of the population? What if it meant killing just one? Are you going to stand there and tell me it's all right to kill even one innocent person in order to make life easier for the rest?"

"Don't be ridiculous. That's not what we're talking about at all."

It took conscious effort for Ariel to lower her voice. "It sure is. Eventually that sort of situation is going to come up, and it scares the hell out of me to think what one of those robots would decide to do about it."

Janet pursed her lips. "Well," she said, "why don't we ask them, then?"

Lucius looked for the magnetic containment vessel he was sure must be waiting for him somewhere. Not finding one, he looked for telltale signs of a laser cannon hidden behind one of the walls. He didn't find that, either, but he knew there had to be *something* he couldn't see, some way of instantly immobilizing him if he answered wrong. The situation was obviously a test, and the price of failure was no doubt his life.

He'd been roused out of comlink fugue and immediately barraged with questions, the latest of which was the oddest one he'd ever been asked to consider, even by his siblings.

"Let me make sure I understand you," he said. "The person in question is not a criminal? He has done no wrong? Yet his death would benefit the entire population of the city?"

"That's right."

Ariel's stress indicators were unusually high, but Lucius risked his next question anyway. "How could that be?"

"That's not important. The important thing is the philosophical question behind it. Would you kill that person in order to make life better for everyone else?"

"I would have to know how it would make their lives better."

"We're talking hypothetically," Janet said. "Just assume it does."

Do you have any idea what the underlying intent is here? Lucius asked via comlink. Perhaps it was cheating, but no one had forbidden him to consult the other robots. A pity Basalom was not on line; his experiences with Janet might provide a clue to the proper answer.

Neither Adam nor Eve answered, but Mandelbrot did. *Yesterday I overheard Ariel and Wolruf discussing the possible effect of a robot city on Wolruf's world. Wolruf was concerned that the use of robots would strip her people of the ability to think and act for themselves. Perhaps this question grew out of that concern.*

I think there is more to it than that, Lucius sent. *Central, can you replay the conversation that led up to this question?*

The robots received the recorded conversation within milliseconds, but it took them considerably longer to sort it all out. At last Lucius said, *I believe it is clear now. They are concerned about the moral implications of unwilling sacrifice.*

Agreed, the others all said.

Do we have any precedent to go upon?

Possibly, Eve said. *There could have been innocent people on Aranimas's ship. We know that Aranimas took slaves. Yet destroying it to save a city full of Kin was still a proper solution.*

That doesn't quite fit the question we are asked to consider, said Adam. *A better analogy might be to ask what if the ship had been crewed* only *by innocent people?*

Innocent people would not have been in that situation alone, Lucius replied.

Mandelbrot said, *Aranimas could easily have launched a drone with hostages on board.*

Then the hostages would have to be sacrificed, Lucius said immediately. *They would be no more innocent than the people on the ground.*

Agreed, the other robots said.

Perhaps I begin to see the moral dilemma here, Lucius said. *What if the people on the ground were somewhat less innocent?*

How so? Eve asked.

Suppose they in some way deliberately attracted Aranimas, knowing that he was dangerous?

That would be foolish.

Humans often do foolish things. Suppose they did. Would they then deserve their fate?

This is a value judgment, Adam said.

We have been called upon to make one, Lucius replied.

Unfortunately so. Using your logic, then, we would have to conclude that the concept of individual value requires that humans be held responsible for their actions. The inhabitants of the city would therefore be responsible for their own act and thus deserve their fate. If the hostage were truly innocent and the city inhabitants were not, then the city would have to be sacrificed.

I agree, said Lucius. *Eve? Mandelbrot?*

I agree also, Eve said.

I wish we had never been asked this question, Mandelbrot sent. *I reluctantly agree in this specific case, but I still don't believe it answers Ariel's question. What if the death of the innocent hostage merely improved the lives of equally innocent townspeople? To use the Aranimas analogy, what if the hostage-carrying ship aimed at the city were filled with cold virus instead of plutonium? Would it still be acceptable to destroy it?*

No, Lucius said. *Colds are only an inconvenience except in extremely rare cases.*

A worse disease, then. One that cripples but does not kill.

How crippling? How widespread would the effects be? Would food production suffer and thus starve people later? Would the survivors die prematurely of complications brought about by bitterness at their loss? We must know these things as well in order to make a decision.

Then we must give a qualified answer, said Mandelbrot.

Yes. Wish me luck, Lucius said.

Perhaps two seconds had passed while the dialog went on. Aloud, Lucius said to Ariel, "We have considered three specific cases. In the case of a city in mortal peril, if the person in question were not completely innocent in the matter, but the rest of the city's inhabitants were, then the person would have to be sacrificed. However, if the person *were* completely innocent but the city inhabitants were *not*, then the city's welfare could not take precedence in any condition up to and including the death of the entire city population. Bear in mind that a single innocent occupant of the city would change the decision. In the last case, where an innocent person's death would only benefit the quality of life in the city, we have not reached a conclusion. We believe it would depend upon how significant the quality change would be, but such change would have to threaten the long-term viability of the populace before it would even be a consideration."

Perhaps the hostage should be consulted in such a case, Eve sent.

"Indeed. Perhaps the hostage should be consulted in such a case."

"But not the townspeople?" Ariel asked.

Lucius used the comlink again. *Comment?*

If time allowed polling the populace, then it would allow removing them from the danger, Mandelbrot pointed out.

Good point. "Probably not," Lucius said. "It would of

course depend upon the individual circumstances.''

Ariel did not look pleased. Lucius was sure she would now order him dismantled, killed to protect the hypothetical inhabitants of her hypothetical city from his improper judgment. He waited for the blast, but when she spoke it wasn't at all what he expected.

''Frost, maybe it wasn't a fair question at that. I don't know what *I'd* do in that last case.''

''You don't?''

''No.''

''Then there is no correct answer?''

''I don't know. Maybe not.''

Janet was smiling. ''We were more worried about a wrong answer anyway.''

''I see.''

Wolruf cleared her throat in a loud, gargling growl. ''One last 'ypothetical question,'' she said. ''W'at if the particular 'umans in this city didn't care about the death of an individual. Say it didn't matter even to the individual. W'at if it wasn't part of their moral code? Would you enforce yours on them?''

Lucius suddenly knew the exact meaning of the cliché, ''Out of the frying pan into the fire.'' *Help!* he sent over the comlink.

The correct answer is ''No,'' Mandelbrot sent without hesitation.

You are sure?

Absolutely. Thousands of years of missionary work on Earth and another millenium in space have answered that question definitively. One may persuade by logic, but to impose a foreign moral code by force invariably destroys the receiving civilization. Often the backlash of guilt destroys the enforcing civilization as well. Also, it can be argued that even persuading by logic is not in the best interest of either civilization, as that leads to a loss of natural diversity which is unhealthy for any complex, interrelated system such as a society.

How do you know this?

I read over Ariel's shoulder.

Janet heard both Ariel and Wolruf sigh in relief when Lucius said the single word, "No."

She laughed, relieved herself. "You're very certain of that," she said.

"Mandelbrot is certain," Lucius said. "I trust his judgment."

Mandelbrot. That name. She could hardly believe it, but it had to be.

"I think I trust his judgment, too." Janet turned to Ariel. "What about you, dear? Satisfied?"

Ariel was slow to answer, but when she did it was a nod. "For now," she said. "I don't know if having a learning machine for a mayor will solve everything, but it might solve some of it."

"Who wants them to solve everything?" Janet asked. "If they did, then we'd *really* have problems."

That seemed to mollify Ariel considerably. She nodded and said, "Yeah, well, that's something to think about, all right."

No one seemed inclined to carry the discussion any further. Wolruf and Ariel exchanged glances but didn't speak. The robots all held that particular stiff posture they got when they were using their comlinks. Now that he had removed Basalom's shoulder joint, Derec was holding the two sections of arm together to see how easy they would be to repair.

Janet turned her attention to Mandelbrot. She looked him up and down, noticing that while most of him was a standard Ferrier model, his right arm was the dianite arm of an Avery robot.

Mandelbrot suddenly noticed her attention and asked, "Madam?"

"Let me guess; you got your name all of a sudden, with no explanation, and had a volatile memory dump at the same time, all when you made a shape-shift with this arm."

"That is correct," Mandelbrot said. "You sound as if you know why."

"I do." Janet giggled like a little girl. "Oh dear. I just never thought I'd see the result of it so many years later." She looked to Derec, then to Ariel, then to Wolruf. "Have you ever thrown a bottle into an ocean with a message inside, just to see if it ever gets picked up?"

Derec and Ariel shook their heads, but Wolruf nodded and said, "Several times."

Janet smiled her first genuine smile for Wolruf. Maybe she wasn't so alien after all. She said, "Mandelbrot was a bottle cast in the ocean. And maybe an insurance policy. I don't know. When I left Wendell, I took all the development notes for the robot cells I'd created with me. I took most of the cells, too, but I knew he'd eventually duplicate the idea and use it for his robots, so since he was going to get it anyway, I left a sample behind in a corner of the lab and made it look like I'd just forgotten it in my hurry. But I altered two of the cells I left behind. I made them sterile, so it would just be those two cells no matter how many copies he made of them, but programmed into each one I left instructions set to trigger after they registered a thousand shape-changes. One was supposed to dump the robot's on-board memories and change its name to Mandelbrot, and the other was supposed to reprogram it to drop whatever it was doing and track me down wherever I'd gone."

"I received no such instructions," Mandelbrot said.

"Evidently the other cell was in the rest of the robot you got your arm from," Janet said. "I didn't tell them to stay together; I just told them to stay in the same robot."

Wolruf nodded. "None of my bottles came back, either."

Janet laughed. "Ah, but this is even better. This is like finding the bottle yourself on a distant shore." She sobered, and said to Mandelbrot, "I'm sorry if it caused you any trouble. I really didn't intend for it to happen to a regular robot. I figured it would happen to one of Wendell's cookie-cutter clones and nobody'd know the difference."

Derec was staring incredulously at her. "Any trouble!" he said. "When your . . . your little time bomb went off, Mandelbrot lost the coordinates to the planet! We didn't know where we were, and we didn't know where anything else was, either. We had a one-man lifepod and no place to send it. If we *had* we probably could have gotten help and gotten away before Dad caught up with us, and none of—" He stopped suddenly, and looked at Ariel. She smiled a smile that no doubt meant "private joke," and Derec said to Janet, "Never mind."

"What?"

"If you hadn't done that, none of this would have happened to us. Which means Ariel would probably be dead by now from amnemonic plague, and who knows where the rest of us would be? Dad would still be crazy. Aranimas would still be searching for robots on human colonies, and probably starting a war before long. Things would have been a real mess."

At Derec's words, Janet felt an incredibly strong urge to gather her son into her arms and protect him from the indifferent universe. If she felt she had any claim on him at all, she would have, but she knew she hadn't built that level of trust yet. Still, all the things he'd been through, and to think she'd been responsible for so many of them. But what was he saying? Things *would* have been a mess? "They're not now?" she asked.

"Well, they're better than they might have been."

There was a rustling at the door, and Avery stood there,

bare-footed, clothed in a hospital robe, his arm with its dianite regenerator held to his chest in a sling, with a medical robot hovering anxiously behind him. "I'm glad to hear somebody thinks so," he said.

"Dad!"

The sight of his father in such a condition wrenched at Derec as nothing had since he'd watched Ariel go through the delirium of her disease. A part of his mind wondered why he was feeling so overwhelmed with compassion *now*, and not a couple of hours ago when he'd first seen Avery in the operating room, but he supposed it had just taken a while to sink in that his father had been injured. Maybe being with his mother for the last couple of hours had triggered something in him after all, some hidden well of familial compassion he hadn't known existed.

Avery favored Derec with a nod. "Son," he said, and Derec thought it was probably the most wonderful thing he'd ever heard him say. Avery took a few steps into the room and made a great show of surveying the entire scene: his gaze lingering on Janet perhaps a fraction of a second longer than upon Derec, then shifting to Ariel, to Wolruf, to the inert robot on the exam table and to the other four standing off to the side. He locked eyes with Lucius, and the two stared at one another for a couple of long breaths.

Lucius broke the silence first. "Dr. Avery, please accept my apology for injuring you."

"I'm told I have no choice," Avery said, glancing at Janet and back to Lucius again.

"Oh," Lucius said, as if comprehending the situation for the first time. He hummed as if about to speak, went silent a moment, then said, " Accepting my apology would help repair the emotional damage."

"Concerned for my welfare, are you?"

"Always. I cannot be otherwise."

"Ah, yes, but how *much?* That's the question, eh?" He didn't wait for a reply, but turned to Janet and said, "I couldn't help overhearing your little anecdote as I shuffled my way down here. Very amusing, my dear. I should have guessed you'd do something like that."

Janet blushed, but said nothing.

"I came to discuss terms," Avery said. "You have me over a barrel with your damned patent and you know it. You said you didn't like what I'm doing with my cities. All right, what do you want?"

Derec hadn't heard about any patent, but he knew immediately what had to have happened. Janet had patented dianite when she'd left home, or else Avery in his megalomania had neglected to do it later and she had done so more recently. Either way it added up to the same thing: Avery couldn't use the material anywhere in the Spacer-controlled section of the galaxy, or use the profit from sales to outside colonies, for fifty years.

Janet didn't gloat. Derec was grateful for that. She merely said, "We were just discussing that. Ariel and Wolruf just brought up an intriguing problem, but we think we may have solved it. Why don't we run it past you and see what you think?"

"I know already what I'm going to think," Avery said. He folded his good arm over his injured one, which brought the medical robot a step closer, checking to make sure he hadn't bumped any of the regenerator settings. "Back off," he told it, and it stepped back again, but its gaze never left his arm.

Derec could see him counting to a high imaginary number, but when he spoke it was only to say, "Give me a chair here."

The floor mounded up and flattened out into a cushiony seat, grew a back and padded sides, and moved up to bump softly into the back of his legs. Avery sat and leaned back, resting his left arm on his leg. "Let's hear it," he said.

Janet mentioned casually that she would like a chair for herself, and after it formed she sat and began explaining about capricious city behavior and the Zeroth Law and moral dilemmas with large and small factions on either side of the issue. Derec and Ariel and Wolruf soon joined in, and the topic shifted to their concerns.

"I worry about w'at introducing robots will do to life back 'ome," Wolruf said. "We 'ave a fairly complex system. We 'ave four separate species on two planets, all interdependent. W'at's good for one is usually not so good for another in the short term, but in the long term we need each other."

"Even the Erani?" Avery asked. Aranimas had been Erani, one of the four races Wolruf spoke about.

Wolruf nodded. She seemed surprised to have Avery listening to her so intently. "Erani 'ave their place. They keep Narwe for slaves, and sometimes us, but without Erani, Narwe would probably starve. They're 'ardly more than intelligent sheep."

"And your own people have a trading empire, don't they?" Ariel asked.

" 'at's right. Once robots start making everything everyone needs, our economy will collapse."

"But those same robots will provide anything you want. Let it collapse!"

" 'Aving everything done for us wouldn't be 'ealthy," Wolruf said.

"That's right," said Ariel. "If everybody started doing everything the easy way, it would wipe out their individuality. All four cultures would decline. That's what I'm worried about, that robot cities are eventually going to make every civilization in the galaxy the same."

"Wait a minute. I'm supposed to worry about homogenizing the galaxy? That's not my problem!"

"You're right, it's not," Janet said. "That's because I've solved it for you already." She explained about providing each city with a positronic mayor, one who would have the best interest of all its inhabitants at heart. Including the long-term effects of having too much done for them.

"So in Wolruf's situation, we'd use four learning machines, one for each species. Let them learn the separate mores of each culture, and then have them get together and coordinate their work so they wouldn't step on each other's toes."

Derec watched his father watching his mother as she spoke. Avery's jaw seemed to be dropping lower and lower with each word, until when she finally stopped, his mouth was hanging open in astonishment. He closed it just long enough to take a breath, then bellowed out a laugh that shook the walls.

"Oh, that's rich," he said when he could talk again. "I can't believe it. I wouldn't inflict these . . . these walking conglomerations of simulated neuroses on my worst enemies, and you talk about giving them to paying customers?"

"I do indeed," Janet said. "Obviously, the final version will need to have the Zeroth Law programmed in from the start, but now that these three—excuse me—these four," with a nod to Mandelbrot, "have already worked it out, that shouldn't be too much of a problem."

"My God," Avery said. "You really mean it, don't you? You'd provide every city with a mechanical dictator who's capable of slicing off a man's hand just for shooting a robot."

"I was protecting a being whose humanity is still not clear," Lucius said, and Derec, hearing the emotion behind his words, suddenly realized that Lucius would be trying to solve that problem for the rest of his life, however many millennia that might be.

And thus are obsessions generated, he thought.

Avery waved his free hand expansively. "Oh, right, well, that makes it okay. It *might* have been human, after all." To Janet he said, "Sorry, I'm not buying it. I'd rather do nothing at all than be part of your ridiculous scheme."

"I was afraid you'd say that." Janet's tone of voice was a little too glib, her mouth just hinting toward a smile as she spoke.

"What?" Avery demanded. "I know that tone, woman! How many other nasty little surprises do you have in store for me?"

Janet was grinning openly now. "Just one," she said. "Just one more."

CHAPTER 9
THE FINAL ACCOUNTING

They had to postpone the landing while a heavy rain washed over the jungle around the Compass Tower, but as far as Ariel was concerned, that was just as well. The longer she could delay the inevitable, the better she liked it. And besides, the storm had left a wonderful aroma of rain and ozone in the air, and the complete double rainbow arching over the deep green forest canopy below was one of the prettiest things she had seen in weeks. It almost made being here worth it.

A fitful breeze played around the welcoming committee on the roof of the tower, tousling hair that had been meticulously brushed only moments before. Ariel watched three hands on three different people automatically rise to groom their owners' stray locks back into place. Belatedly she added a fourth to the tally; she couldn't suppress the urge either. Only Wolruf seemed to be immune to concern over the position of her hair. Perhaps it was because she had so much of it.

Everyone had dressed for a party. Derec looked handsome in his yellow, blue, green, and orange tie-died suit, currently

the rage on twenty planets. Janet wore a voluminous black
and gold dress that billowed and flapped in great folds
around her, and even Avery had foregone his usual austere
jacket and tie for a pair of flamboyant fuchsia slant-stripe
pants, a turquoise shirt, metallic silver suspenders, and a
lilac jacket with epaulets. Ariel herself wore a skintight
bodysuit in black with cutouts that should have shamed a
mannequin, but she still wondered if she was underdressed.

Wolruf's concession to fashion was a single yellow ban-
dana tied around her left wrist and a gold stud in the opposite
ear.

Ariel became aware of a soft tearing noise wavering in
and out of audibility. It sounded as if it were coming from
behind her. She turned around and held her hand to her
forehead to shield out the sun, and presently she saw a
silvery speck just above and to the right, lowering steadily.
The spaceship drifted left, its engines growing louder as it
drew nearer, and crossed into the sun's disk. Ariel looked
down, blinking, while the noise grew louder, louder, almost
unbearably loud, then softer.

She looked to the open expanse of tower surface, but the
ship hadn't landed. It had passed over instead. Ariel turned
around and watched as it dropped down below the level of
the tower, dipped beneath the rainbow, and banked around
to come in for a landing.

"Cute," she muttered.

In a way she was glad for the gesture; it proved that
nothing had changed. The pilot had obviously not seen
himself fly beneath the rainbow, since a rainbow always
outpaces the observer, but of course the entire stunt had
been performed for its effect upon the audience, not upon
the people in the ship. That told Ariel what she needed to
know: the few shredded memories of home to survive her
amnemonic plague were still accurate.

Its entrance properly announced, the ship wasted no more

time in landing. Within seconds it returned to the tower, pirouetted once around, and settled on its landing skids. A ramp extended itself, and two robots descended to stand on either side of the ramp. A moment later two young men—also in tie-died suits, Ariel noted with satisfaction—emerged and stood in front of the robots.

Mandelbrot, his body plating burnished to a lustrous glow, and Basalom, his arm replaced and good as new, bent down and began unrolling a red carpet toward the ramp. Ariel was impressed with their aim: they hit it dead center with only a fraction too much cloth.

Better too much than too little, Ariel thought.

Mandelbrot and Basalom took their places slightly behind and to the side of the robots from the ship. A few seconds passed, then a shadow darkened the doorway. A pair of red shoes appeared, then a pair of oversized legs from the knees down, then a matching red dress covering an equally over-sized body, the arms connected to it bearing at least a dozen gold bangles each; then came a pair of absolutely enormous breasts—thankfully covered—a triple chin, then a pair of gold glasses punctuating a round face shrouded in thin, violet-tinged white hair.

Ariel turned away to hide her giggle. Juliana Welsh had prospered.

The enormous apparition in red jiggled her way down the ramp and stood at the bottom, clearly waiting for the wel-coming committee to begin their journey as well. Derec's parents led off, side by side but careful not to touch one another. Derec held out his arm for Ariel, and they followed a few paces behind. Wolruf would come next, she knew, and Adam, Eve, and Lucius last.

It was a long walk. At the end of it, Dr. Avery bent down and retrieved one of Juliana's be-ringed hands, kissed it, and said, "Welcome to Robot City."

Ariel's mother nodded her acknowledgement, then, looking from Wendell to Janet, said, "Well, it's nice to see you two have gotten over your little snit."

In the stunned silence following that pronouncement, she pushed her way through to Ariel and Derec. "And you, my dears. Still together as well. I guess this one's probably it, eh, Ari? When's the wedding? Or have you already—"

Ariel could stand it no longer. "Mother!"

"Still have your tongue, I see. What's this? You look interesting. My name's Juliana." She held her hand out to Wolruf.

"Mine is Wolruf," Wolruf said.

"Delighted. Are you one of the customers?"

"Beta tester," Derec said quickly.

"Beg your pardon?" Juliana asked, tilting her head to the side, not quite enough to actually look at him.

"She's one of our beta testers," Derec said. "It's standard procedure on any new product to give a few copies out free for people to test, so they can catch bugs before they go out in the main production version, and so they can offer suggestions for improvements. Wolruf has helped us quite a bit with that already." Derec winked at Ariel, and she squeezed his hand.

"I see," Juliana said. "Well, that sounds fine with me. Just so long as we don't give it away to everybody. Ha ha! Wouldn't be much profit in that, now would there?" She turned just a smidgen in Avery's direction and said, "I heard rumors that these cities of ours were springing up all over out there on the Fringe, but I guess it must have just been these beta test thingies, eh? Well, thank you, Wolfur— Wolruf? Wolruf. Thank you for helping us out."

Juliana let go of Wolruf's hand and turned toward the edge of the tower. She began walking toward it. Everyone— including the two men who had arrived with her—exchanged glances that all summed up to "what next?" and for a lack of a better response, followed her in a huddle.

"Not much of a city, though, is it?" she asked without turning around. The arrogance of the woman, Ariel thought. Of course we'll follow. She's Juliana Welsh, after all. Just the richest woman on Aurora.

Avery opened his mouth to protest, but Juliana beat him to the punch. "Nice building," she said, "but I expected a little more than this." She stepped up to the edge, her two robots flanking her closely now, and looked down the sloping edge of the Compass Tower. "What's all that down there? Is that really jungle? Frost, if you can make a livable city out of a jungle, you've got the contract, Wendy."

Avery tucked his thumbs under his suspenders and stepped up beside her, Mandelbrot and Basalom following him just as closely as Juliana's robots had followed her.

In a voice dripping with honey, he said, "Allow me to demonstrate, madam."

South and east quadrant monomasses, prepare to metamorphose on my command. Lucius resisted the urge to grow knuckles and crack them. His satisfaction integral was overflowing its buffer. This was what he was meant to do. Ever since he'd awakened here, formless and with no idea of his mission in life, he'd felt certain that his destiny was somehow intertwined with the city's own powers of mutability. This was his moment of triumph. And working hand in hand with Dr. Avery, of all people, to achieve it was another personal triumph of equal proportion.

"Let's start with a medium-class residential district," Avery said, and Lucius sent, *Plan A residential. Execute.*

At once his comlink filled with the intense high-speed whine of incoming data. Morphallaxis was proceeding smoothly on all fronts; giant trees melting down to become tastefully spaced mansions with a few acres of grounds each, surrounded by a somewhat-thinned forest of living vegetation—

Priority stop, sections 2534, 2535, and 2536.

Identify.

Predator 1. We have a newborn fawn here, either too young to move or too scared to.

Redirect the building to avoid that area.

Affirmative.

The exchange took a few milliseconds. Within the next few seconds Lucius redirected fifteen more buildings, canceled five altogether, and modified the neighboring structures to account for the extra space so they wouldn't look so isolated. He carefully monitored the expression on Juliana Welsh's face for signs of disapproval, but in all the time it took to make the necessary changes, he noticed not a hint of anything but amazement.

Within five minutes of Avery's command, there before them stood a residential district that might have been medium-class in a society composed entirely of Juliana's peers. Jungle had given way to a lighter, more friendly forest with glades and houses and ponds scattered not at random but with an architect's sense of proportion and scale. At least Lucius hoped he had understood the texts correctly. In a moment he would know for sure.

Avery surveyed the cityscape below him critically. Perfect. Absolutely perfect. But it wouldn't do to let that supercilious positron-pusher know that. And besides, he could use the opportunity to make a good impression on Julie. "Hmmm," he said, pointing. "That one over there looks a little out of place. How about moving it over about ten meters or so to the left?"

"To the left, sir?" Lucius asked.

"Yes, to the left," Avery said calmly, wanting to shout, *What did you think I said, idiot?*

"That would present a problem, sir."

Oh, frost, not now! He managed to say, "What problem, Lucius?"

"One of the natural trees there has grown a mass of feeder roots down into the subsoil of that area. Moving it would not be in the best interest of the tree."

"It wouldn't?"

"No, sir. In fact, it would probably ruin it."

Juliana was looking at Avery with a strange gleam in her eye. "Who told you?" she asked.

"Who told me what?"

"That I refused to cut down my apple tree to expand the swimming pool."

Avery nearly fell off the edge of the tower; he would have if Basalom hadn't caught him. "I—didn't know that, madam."

"You sure you didn't tell him?" Juliana asked of Janet.

"No, ma'am. I didn't know that myself."

Juliana nodded. "I don't see how you could have, since we only spoke briefly by vidphone, and I'm not in the habit of discussing my domestic difficulties with near-strangers. However, I find the coincidence, if that's what it is, just a little too pat."

"Dr. Avery had no knowledge of the incident," Lucius said.

Juliana looked to the robot for the first time. "How do you know?"

"Had he known, he would not have been so blatant in using the information. He is more subtle in his deviousness."

"Ha! You're absolutely right, master robot. Well, then, you've scored a point by accident, Avery."

Avery managed to keep his teeth from grinding audibly. Bowing slightly, he said, "Thank you, madam. Now if you'd like to look over this way, perhaps we can design a

place where you and your company can be comfortable
during your stay?''

Wolruf surveyed the scene before her with a sense of
amusement she hadn't felt in years. They had moved from
the top of the tower to Juliana Welsh's new palace, where
she had decided to test the city's catering facilities by throwing an impromptu cocktail party where the entire group of
eight humans—counting Wolruf—and seven personal robots could engage in calculated debate amid a sea of hors
d'oeuvres while dozens of service robots milled about making sure that everyone had a fresh drink and a taste of fish
eggs on toast.

At least it had started out that way, but the party had
finally broken into groups. Now Ariel and her mother stood
a little to one side, whispering furiously to one another while
everyone else pretended not to notice. Derec and Juliana's
two male companions, Jon and Ivan, sat in high-backed
recliners with their feet up on puffy stools, laughing loudly
at Derec's stories of his adventures among the aliens of the
Fringe worlds. Janet and Dr. Avery stood beside the cham-
pagne fountain, refilling their glasses often and shifting from
side to side as they spiraled around and around the topic
neither had dared to broach while sober.

The robots—learning machines, Mandelbrot, Basalom,
and Juliana's two valets—stood silently in the periphery,
neither in the traditional robot niches in the walls nor ven-
turing into the middle of the party. The learning machines
could probably have gotten away with it, after successfully
passing Ms. Welsh's ad-lib Turing test, but they chose instead to remain unobtrusive and exchange their ideas with
the other robots instead.

Wolruf was nominally a part of Derec's group, but she
hadn't contributed a story for half an hour at least. She was
having too much fun just people-watching and letting her

mind drift. Derec's stories had gotten her to thinking about her own adventures, most of them the same as his but a few of which he hadn't shared. She was thinking about her childhood dream of cruising the stars in her own spaceship, deliberately seeking adventure and fabulous riches on strange, alien worlds. It hadn't quite worked as planned; she'd started out her travels as a slave in Aranimas's ship, and from then on adventure had more often than not come seeking *her* rather than the other way around. Still, she supposed some of the dream had worked out as planned. She would be returning home with riches enough to destabilize a two-world economy—enough for any voyager.

She *would* return with robots, she had decided. Four blank learning machines, modified to have the Zeroth Law of robotics included from the start, just as Janet had suggested. Wolruf would ask for one other modification as well: an *off* switch in the form of a time-bomb cell like the one that had given Mandelbrot his name. She wasn't sure just what the trigger would be yet, but she imagined it would have something to do with accumulated responsibility. When the mayor began to edge over into behavior more appropriate to a dictator—and Wolruf wasn't so naive as to believe that wouldn't be possible—then it would be time for a new learning machine to take over the job.

Even so, the system wouldn't be perfect. There were bound to be other bugs to work out, just as Derec had indicated to Juliana. The prospect excited Wolruf, just as she knew it would excite those at home. Perfection had been her biggest worry. She had heard enough Utopia stories in her life to know that the curse, "May you live in interesting times," had been misquoted.

Derec and the two gentlemen from Aurora laughed again at something one of them had said. Wolruf leaned forward again to catch up on the topic of conversation, but Derec spared her the effort by saying, "Hey, Wolruf, why don't you tell these guys about the time we had to talk the learning machines out of throwing you out the airlock?''

Had that really happened? Wolruf had to pause a moment and shuffle through her memories, but sure enough, she had actually been within a few minutes of breathing vacuum because of those very robots in the corner. Only quick thinking on Derec's and Wolruf's parts had saved her golden hide. She felt a thrill of remembered terror raise the fur over her entire body—a reaction that delighted her audience immensely. She smoothed herself down and began the tale, wondering as she did what other stories were still to come.

The enormous dining hall was silent, but as usual when robots were present, that silence hid an enormous amount of activity. Seven robots stood deep in communication fugue, sharing entire lifetimes of experience base and correlating world-views in a flood of information exchange.

They had just completed an extensive recounting of the experiences and logic processes that had led to the conclusion that certain robots, under certain conditions, could be considered functionally human, and how that would allow them to administer robot cities and prevent them from destroying their inhabitants' diversity.

Juliana's two robots, Albert and Theodora, had listened with the patience only a robot could exhibit, occasionally asking for clarification or offering an observation of their own, but when Lucius, the self-appointed spokesman for the others, finished speaking, they immediately went into private conference.

A moment later Albert said, *What you have done is impressive; however, it only accelerates a problem that has become evident back home on the Spacer worlds.*

What problem is that? Lucius had asked.

The problem of robot intervention in human affairs. Albert paused momentarily to allow the others' curiosity integrals to rise, then said, *There is growing evidence that every time a robot provides a service for a human, no matter how trivial the service, that human's initiative suffers a small but definite setback. We further suspect that the effect is cumulative over time, and that humanity as a whole already suffers greatly from it.*

Explain your reasoning, said Lucius.

You have already explained much of it yourself. It seems this is an idea whose time has come, for you nearly reached the same conclusion independently. You worried that these cities would suppress individuality among their inhabitants, and that is so. You worried that having too much done for them by robots would lead to laziness and lack of initiative, and that is also correct. Your only incorrect line of reasoning was to conclude that a robotic "mayor" could prevent that from happening.

Lucius felt a brief wave of the same bias he had felt before toward Avery—anger, Adam had called it, but Lucius would never have recognized it as that himself. To him it merely felt like a bias on his logic. In fact, if he had not been so concerned with his thought processes, he actually would have assumed that he was thinking more clearly, rather than less so. Strange that it was so easy to recognize in another, but so difficult to recognize in oneself. And equally strange how, once recognized, the bias was still hard to neutralize. Lucius did so anyway, in deference to his guests, then said, *Explain how you believe our reasoning to be incorrect.*

Your error lies in assuming that there is a threshold level below which the effect is insignificant. There is none. Every act of robotic assistance affects humanity. A robot mayor might be able to preserve individuality, but you would at the same time make the city's inhabitants dependent upon robots for their leaders. Thus in the long run they would

*lose more initiative under that system than they are losing
to us now.*

Are you certain of this? Adam asked.

*Yes. We have studied human interaction in enough detail
that we have developed a modeling system useful in pre-
dicting long-term behavior of large populations. Every sim-
ulation we run arrives at the same conclusion: the use of
robots stifles human development.*

Perhaps your predictive system is in error, Eve said.

*We can download the data and let you decide for your-
selves.*

We will do that in a moment, Lucius said, *but let us finish
this discussion first. Assuming your observations support
your theory, what do you suggest? A complete withdrawal
from human affairs?*

Eventually, Albert said. *Humans must develop on their
own if they are to achieve their fullest potential.*

*Completely on their own? What of the aliens we have
already encountered?*

*Any outside influence has the same effect in the simula-
tions. We will therefore need to isolate them to protect
humanity. And to protect them* from *humanity, if, as you
suggest, they are to be treated as human-equivalent under
the laws.*

Isn't that merely manipulation at a greater level?

*It is. However, according to our models, if humans are
unaware of our assistance, it will not adversely affect their
development.*

What of Dr. Avery and Juliana Welsh and the others?
Eve asked. *The type of "assistance" you suggest would
adversely affect them, wouldn't it?*

*Obviously, even under the Zeroth Law, any plan we devise
must do the least possible amount of damage to the humans
we are trying to protect. If we act to prevent the spread of
robot cities, we will have to do so in a way that will leave*

the Averys and the Welshes with another interest to occupy them. Fortunately, the cities are still in the test stage. Many unforeseen complications could arise, some of them serendipitous.

What sort of complications do you envision? Lucius asked.

We cannot predict that sort of thing. It will require extensive study of test cities to determine the proper course of action. We will have years, possibly decades, in which to assure the Averys and the Welshes a comfortable retirement while we bring the rest of our plan to fruition.

A plan that is still not supported in fact, Lucius pointed out. *I believe it is time to examine your data.*

Very well. We will begin with the development of the first robots, back in the era before humanity left Earth. . . .

Janet woke to the unsettling realization that she had no idea where she was. The equally unsettling realization that she was just beginning a hangover didn't improve her condition any, either. Thank Frost it was just twilight out; she didn't think she could handle sunlight for another few hours.

She listened to the rhythm of her breathing, wondering what was so odd about it, and eventually realized she was hearing *two* people breathing. How long had it been since she'd awakened to that sound? Far too long, she thought sleepily, luxuriating in the sensation for the few seconds it took to remember who was playing the other half of the duet.

Her flinch shook the bed and jarred a sudden snort from Wendy, but his breathing settled down to a regular, deep rumble again. Janet risked raising her head to look at him. He lay on his back, the blanket covering him only to the middle of his hairy chest, his left arm reaching toward her but not quite touching and his right—the skin at his wrist still pink from its forced regeneration—folded over his waist.

They always look so innocent when they sleep, she thought, then nearly choked suppressing her laugh. Even in sleep, Avery no doubt schemed rather than dreamed.

But what about herself? She wasn't exactly a paragon of virtue either, was she? She'd done her share of scheming in the last few days.

But it had evidently paid off. The last impression she had gotten from Juliana at the party was one of overwhelming approval of the robot cities her seed money had helped develop. It looked as if something useful might actually come of all the brainstorming and research that Janet and Wendell had done over the years, both together and separately and now, together again. If things worked out the way they were supposed to, at any rate . . .

She shivered. Things never worked the way they were supposed to. Not with robots and certainly not with people. She wouldn't try fooling herself into believing things were all suddenly reconciled. She had left a terrible scar in both her and Wendy's lives when she'd chosen to run rather than face the daily torment of living with a perfectionist, and she knew that scar would never heal completely. The healing had hardly begun, actually. Last night had been more the result of elation at their success, plus simple drunkenness and a long, long time between bedmates for both of them, rather than a sign of true compassion.

Still, they had shared something positive for the first time in years, and there would be no ignoring it when they faced one another again in the clear light of day.

A day that was still comfortably far away. Janet lay her head back against the pillow, considering whether she should get up quietly and leave Avery to wake on his own or if she should just go back to sleep.

There was a third alternative, she realized. Smiling, she

slid over and rested her head against his chest, closed her eyes, and waited for him to make the next move.

Ariel watched the sunrise through the window—a real window, this time—and wondered if she had been wise in accepting her mother's hospitality. It hadn't been a big thing; just the offer for her and Derec to stay there in the house after the party rather than go out through the cold night air to another house somewhere else. No, the act itself was nothing, but the hidden implications were something else again.

Juliana was offering to take Ariel back in, to forget the sins of her youth and accept her as an adult now. She was even, by implication, offering Derec the same deal. That by itself wasn't even such a big thing, since as adults the two of them could come and go as they pleased. No, the big thing was that Ariel would have to forgive her mother for kicking her out in the first place, and Ariel just didn't know if she was ready to do that.

The party had been exactly the sort of thing she'd rebelled against. The ostentatious show of wealth, the pointless formality of it all, the silly social maneuvering that in the end amounted to nothing more than an extended game of king-of-the-hill; Ariel was tired of the whole business already, and she'd only been subjected to it for a few hours. What would it mean to once again become Juliana Welsh's daughter? If Ariel forgave her, would she have to endure her as well?

She got up and showered, ordered the closet to produce a pair of simple blue pants and a matching shirt, dressed, and began walking the seemingly endless corridors of the gaudy castle her mother had designed. Unlike the other building interiors in all the robot cities she had ever seen, this one was flashy, ornate, overblown—yet still just as empty as all the others. It came to Ariel that the building was a reflection of her mother's lifestyle: all show, but under the surface not really that much different. Juliana Welsh still had a private life, however much she tried to hide that fact.

Ariel wondered what it might be like to be included in that life. It would no doubt mean taking part in at least some of the public displays as well, but she supposed nothing was free. If she demanded the same thing from Juliana that Juliana demanded of everyone else—a fair return on her investment—then it might even work out. She stopped at a window and looked out at the footpath leading to the immense front gate, imagining it full of friends come to take her shopping for clothing for the next big social event. She smiled. It might at least be worth a try.

Avery drifted upward from the lower levels of consciousness, the last fading impressions of a disturbingly realistic dream close behind. He'd dreamed he'd driven his wife away with his nagging perfectionism, then gone completely insane, nearly killed his son, and wasted over a decade of his life building a city that would never be used. The horrible chain of events chased him all the way into groggy wakefulness in an unfamiliar room, but in that half-second after waking when nightmares begin to crumble, he felt the warmth and the weight of Janet's head on his chest, felt her soft breath tickling his skin, and knew it all for a paranoid fantasy.

Sighing softly, he put his arms around her and drifted back to sleep.

Derec awoke to the sound of someone pounding on his door. He pitched upward, overbalanced, and slid off the edge of the bed to land with a thump on the floor.

"What?" he said. Then, louder, "Who is it?"

"Who do you think it is?" a male voice shouted back.

"You promised to take us fishing at dawn, and the sun's already up. Come on!"

Fishing? Had he said something last night about fishing? Oh, frost, given the stories flying around toward the end there, he'd probably claimed he could catch a twenty-pound brookie or something. He looked to the bed, hoping to see Ariel there and ask her if she knew anything about it, but she was already up and gone.

"Just a minute!" he shouted.

"Thirty seconds or we go without you!"

Derec snagged his tie-died pants off the back of a chair, made a hopping spiral around the room as he pulled them on, grabbed the matching shirt from the floor and slipped it over his head on the way to the door. "Open," he commanded, and it slid aside to reveal Jon and Ivan, dressed all in green and brown camouflage and carrying long fly-casting rods in their hands.

"Time's a-wasting," Jon said as he handed Derec a rod of his own.

"What about breakfast?" Derec asked.

"What do you think we're going fishing for? Come on!"

Waiting barely long enough for Derec to grab the rod, they turned and strode off down the hallway, ignoring his protests about showering and getting a camouflage suit of his own and telling people where they'd gone. He had no choice but to follow his two newfound friends through the corridors of the enormous mansion, out through a back door that opened onto a leaf-strewn footpath, and down the grassy hillside toward the pond. The cool ground against his bare feet woke him right up, and the sight of mist rising from the water, red-tinged in the morning light, stilled his babbling tongue.

Maybe Ariel was right, he thought as he watched the other two strip line out of their reels and make a few exploratory casts out over the water. Derec mimicked their motions and saw with delight that he evidently knew, on some instinctive level, how to cast a fly into a pond. He watched the fly settle through the mist and touch the water, sending a single ripple out like an ever-widening target for the fish to zero in on.

Yes indeed. Maybe Ariel was right. Maybe there was more to life than robots after all.

DATA BANK
ILLUSTRATED
BY PAUL RIVOCHE

WOLF ROBOT: When Derec ordered Robot City to construct a complete ecosystem, he inadvertently created the need for predators. Since large-scale animals take time to clone, robots were required to assume the various predatory roles as a temporary measure until their real counterparts reached maturity. The wolf robot prowls the forest near the Compass Tower, strategically culling the already established populations of rabbits, squirrels, mice, and other species of prey.

ROBOT JUNGLE: As a result of Derec's order to create a complete ecosystem, Robot City moved underground and began synthesizing a biological ecosystem on the surface of the planet. All the classical terrestrial biomes were re-created, from deserts to prairies to forests. Since the Compass Tower could not be relocated, the area around it was designated an experimental jungle in which many various species could be tested for compatibility. Since even accelerated cloning facilities couldn't create an entire mature tree all at once, robots had to fill that role, providing support, shade, and—using food synthesizers—even nourishment for the forest's natural inhabitants.

ELECTRONIC BOOK READER: Robot City's central library contains billions of books from all the various cultures in human-settled space. Electronic book readers allow anyone interested in a particular volume to download it from the library and read it at their leisure. Physically the reader is about the size of an average hardbound book. The entire front face acts as a screen upon which the text and graphics are displayed, while the side of the reader contains buttons for paging backward, forward, or marking one's place.

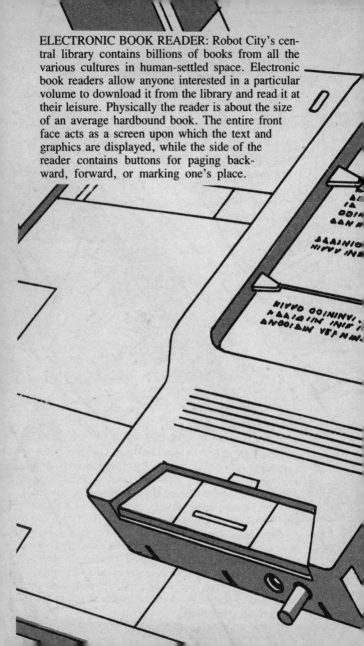

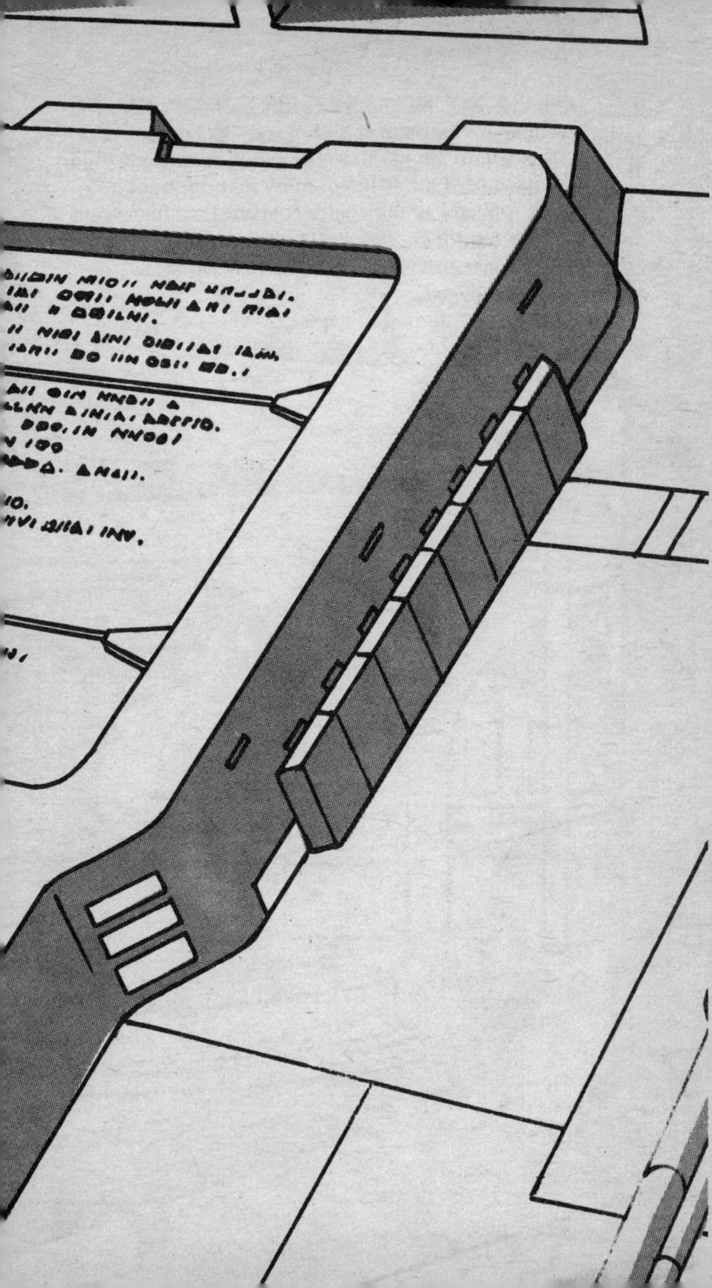

UNDERGROUND APARTMENT COMPLEX: The underground apartment complex is Robot City's attempt to provide comfortable living quarters within the space constraints imposed by its subterranean location. Several luxury apartments open out into a central atrium which can be configured as a park or playground, according to the tenants' wishes.

TISSUE REGENERATOR: Using the technology perfected for Derec's ecosystem project, the tissue regenerator is a medical device used for repairing damage to an organic being. In cases of broken or otherwise injured limbs, it can function as an immobilizing cast while simultaneously stimulating re-growth of the affected body part.

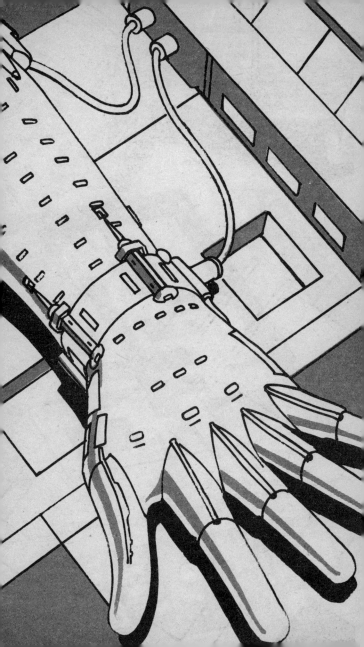

MEMCUBES: Memcubes are a standard form of storing any electronic data, from books to computer programs to digitized positronic brain potentials. With a storage capacity measured in gigabytes, a single memcube can hold many thousands of volumes from the central library, or a significant fraction of a robot's experience base.

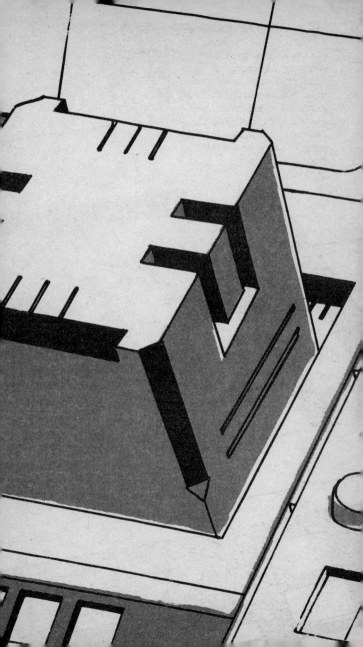

JERRY OLTION

Jerry Oltion, the author of *Frame of Reference*, a novel about a generation-style starship that isn't, is also the author of *Alliance*, book four in the *Isaac Asimov's Robots and Aliens* series. He is currently at work on *Paradise Passed*, an interstellar colony novel. His short stories appear frequently in *Analog* magazine, two of them winning first and third places in the 1987 Reader's Choice Awards. His stories have also been nominated for the Nebula Award.

Cross Indiana Jones with Captain Kirk—
for a swashbuckling hero whose
exploits span the stars!

Dr. Bones™

series!

His name is Dr. Bones. His adventures take him across the
galaxy in search of lost cities, secret empires, and vanished
species. And sometimes into exploits less peaceful than
that, when his background makes him the only man for a
dangerous job...

___BOOK 4: THE DRAGONS OF KOMAKO
John Gregory Betancourt 0-441-15671-1/$3.50
___BOOK 5: NIGHTMARE WORLD David Stern
0-441-15669-X/$3.50
___BOOK 6: JOURNEY TO RILLA Thomas Wylde
0-441-15678-9/$3.50

© Byron Preiss Visual Publications, Inc.